Billy's Goat

By Cynthia Davidson Bend:

Birth of a Modern Shaman
Arthur's Room
Burning Clean

Billy's Goat

CYNTHIA DAVIDSON BEND

YTTERLI PRESS
Saint Paul
2006

ACKNOWLEDGEMENTS

Thank you, Carol Ellingson and Dick Bend for your critiques and editing, contributions surpassed only by "Billy," Dick's goat (a doe), and by "Brighty," Doug's blue jay. Jennifer Bend, thanks for your sinister portrait of "the spook." Thanks, Harold, for your artistic encouragement and your gifted family. Torry, for your expressive illustrations and detailed map. Barb, who read *Billy's Goat* to her third and fourth grade students, and to those students for their enthusiastic comments. Thanks to Katie Rubenstein for her equine knowledge and to Bob Nelson for setting me right on milking machines. Thank you, Meredith, for your willing and constant assistance. Thanks go to Ytterli Press and to Sylvia Ruud, who has given so much artistic talent and personal attention to making *Billy's Goat* as good as it can be.

ISBN 0-9771069-2-6

Published by Ytterli Press
2211 Buford Avenue, Saint Paul, Minnesota 55108

To contact the author: cynthiab@pressenter.com
or write to Ytterli Press at the above address.

Library of Congress Catalog Card Number applied for.

Printed in the United States of America

Book design by Sylvia Ruud
Drawings by Torry Bend and Jennifer Bend

To Ayla Rubenstein
with thanks for her art, her suggestions, and her appreciation

And to Isabelle Warzecha
who will learn to read sooner than we think

Billy's Goat

Chapter 1

"No!"

It was a pretty good day to start with. For his sixth grade class Bill read a story he had written about a goat that guarded a flock of sheep. A strong billy with long horns chased off a coyote just before he grabbed a newborn lamb. Nobody in the whole class knew that a goat would do that, not even his teacher.

The ride home on the school bus was good, too—no thanks to Kim who plopped himself down beside Bill. Nobody much liked Kim. Anyway, Bill didn't want his thoughts interrupted. But Kim started right in—bragging. "I suppose you've heard about the new dog Pa's getting for me?"

"Nope." The bus lurched forward, and Bill turned the back of his head to Kim and watched the clay-colored snowbank speed past the window.

"It's a bulldog that he's going to import from England. Just about top breeding in the world." Kim paused to let his news sink in.

"I'd rather have a goat," Bill said.

"Are you nuts?"

"I can teach my goat more than you'll ever teach your bull-dog. Goats are smart as anything, and they get to like one person just like a good dog."

Kim ruffled like a peacock forced to share a roost with common chickens. "Huh, *Billy*," he pecked. "Even named after a stinking billy goat, aren't you?"

Bill's quiet gray eyes narrowed as he turned them from the snowbank and squinted at Kim from under a shelf of sandy brown hair that stuck out like a visor. He was about to retort when an exclamation hit Kim from the seat behind them.

"Look out, big mouth! No decent goat likes the stink of a conceited skunk." The taunt came from Doug Mason, a lanky boy with curly black hair and a birdlike snap in his dark eyes.

Kim sputtered, then leaned across the aisle to impress a small chick of a girl with downy blond hair.

Doug was a year older than Bill, restless and energetic. He spoke in staccato bursts; his mind and his quick bird-eyes jumped as fast as his words. "What gives on this goat? You really going to get a goat?"

"Sure. In the spring." He just had to believe it himself or it couldn't happen.

As he and Doug talked about Bill's goat, his future pet became more and more certain. "We can teach her to pull a wagon like nothing," Bill said as the bus jolted to a stop in front of Kim's driveway flanked by white rail fences. The house and the long, low barn of Cummings Dairy Farms, Inc. rose gleaming whiter than the snow. Three huge blue-black silos dwarfed the barn. Barely visible beyond the Cummings's barn and fields, Bill could see the shingled peak of his own barn roof, the barn his grandfather built.

"Just 'cause his dad's got the biggest farm in the county, he thinks everyone else should treat him like royalty," Bill muttered over his shoulder to Doug.

"So long, billy goat," Kim mocked as he slid from his seat.

Bill's usually full mouth set in a tight line; his square jaw broadened as he clamped his teeth.

He watched Kim hunch through the snow, and imagined a goat with nice long horns aiming at Kim's broad behind. Kim would roll, oh so solidly, into the snowbank beside the road. Aloud Bill said, "Mr. Cothern sells his doe kids for ten dollars. A buck would be cheaper, but they can get mean as a bull."

"Ten for a good doe. Not bad," Doug responded.

"His are real good. French Alpines. Registered and everything. Would like to get Matilda, but she's about ready to breed, so Mr. Cothern probably wants to keep her for milking."

"You could really make the dough when your kid starts milking."

"Sure could. A lot more than raising moths like that sister of mine."

The bus had turned south to the county road. It crossed a bridge over a small stream, then lurched to a stop. Doug stood up. "I'll help you train her," he tossed over his shoulder as he walked down the aisle. "We'll really have something. Talk about it some more tomorrow." Bill watched his best friend stride up the wooded driveway toward the house hidden by trees. Doug's farm was next to Bill's, but Mr. Mason had quit farming, and now Bill's father worked the Mason farm as well as his own.

At the next stop Bill hopped down from the bus in high spirits. He walked up the snow-packed driveway over the hump that hid the house and barn. His kid brother and sister were behind him. Jane was in fifth grade and Sammy in first.

Bill walked into the yard. His father was running toward the barn, in a hurry as always. Like work'll get away from him if he doesn't grab it by the tail, Bill thought as he ran to catch him.

"Pa," he shouted from across the yard, "Can I have a goat?"

"No, you can not."

That "No!" slammed into Bill's brain and exploded. He stepped back as if he had been hit. That "No!" blew his whole day to pieces.

"But why?"

"You aren't old enough to take care of a goat."

"I'm a whole year older than Jane, and she's always having pets."

"Not goats. Your mother would have to keep it off the car, out of the garden, and off the doorstep."

"But a goat wouldn't be as much trouble as Jane's squirrel was. She let him get on the table, and she kept him in her sleeve when she washed the dishes, and his tail would trail in the water, and then she let him jump into the ketchup kettle and get boiled, and right away she got all those caterpillars, and..."

"Billy, that's enough. A squirrel may be a nuisance, but a goat is destructive."

"But I'd keep her staked."

"Sure as shootin' she'd get loose. Remember those rabbits that starved to death in the basement? Your mother..."

Bill didn't wait for him to finish. In his hurry to leave his whole shattered life behind, he took off at a run, taking a short-cut through last year's cornfield. He rolled under the fence and slid on the seat of his jeans down the bank to the road. A thorn from a blackcap cane snagged his pants where the blue had worn white. His anger spilled over to his mother for letting him wear worn-out pants. He thought of Kim's big, important-looking father always giving stuff to Kim, and then of his own father. Mr. Brock was small and wiry, much stronger than he looked. He didn't know about "All work and no play makes Jack a dull boy." He'd say, "All play and no work makes Jack a jerk." Now that he had a tractor and a milking machine he didn't have to work as hard as he used to during all those hard years of depression and drought, but he did anyway—just took on more land. Bill didn't want Kim's father, but he sure would like it if his own father would give him some respect—and quit calling him "Billy." He had been refused a goat just as if he were still an irresponsible baby. Those rabbits were two years ago. He was almost thirteen now.

With anger hot inside him, Bill started south along the county road. The icy indifference of the skeletal oaks and snow-smoothed fields about him fired his angry disappointment, and Bill had a hard time keeping back the tears.

He had not gone far before he noticed something beside the road ahead of him. Bill brushed his mitten across his eyes with a sense of relief from what was going on inside his head. He focused his attention on the buff-gray mound in the ditch to his right. The lumpy darkness emerging from the snow looked a little like a big rock, but no rock had been there before. For some reason he shivered, spooked, the same way he felt when he met Old Man Crawley on the road or when he saw the two-headed pig displayed in a jar of formaldehyde at the Hudson grain elevator. Perhaps it was only a feed sack that had fallen from a truck and slid down the embankment. Yet it didn't look like a feed sack either. It was too irregular in shape, and now that he was closer, it looked too big.

Bill was almost up to it before he realized what it was. "Crawley's sow!" he exclaimed aloud. She had apparently been struck by a car. Bill prodded the animal's snout with his boot. There was nothing gruesome about the sow: no blood, she was on her side in a natural position. At first she looked as though she were sleeping, but Bill soon saw that her eyes were open, fixed and glassy. One hind leg was sticking up in the air as though she had been frozen in the middle of a kick.

"Why can't that crawling Spook keep his fences fixed?" Bill muttered as he turned away, disgusted and sickened at the careless waste of life.

When he came abreast of Crawley's dilapidated house, he heard men's voices, blurred by the distance. The volume rose, but he couldn't make out their words. He could imagine the

Spook in his loose-fitting overalls and a flapping denim jacket that made his scrawny body look even less substantial than it was.

Bill quickened his steps in his hurry to reach the cheerful and well-kept house and barn of Mr. Rutherford across the road from Crawley's and a little farther south.

When he came to the fence line, Bill heard a car start up, and he looked back. A sleek blue Chrysler turned out of the Crawley place and came up behind Bill. He recognized Mr. Rutherford's car. A strange thing for the dignified lawyer to be visiting the old Spook. As the car passed him, Bill waved, but Mr. Rutherford looked right through him. Bill glimpsed a small dent in the right fender of the car, and he guessed that the visit was about the sow. He watched the Chrysler turn in at the gate across the road, his eyes marking the clean white house and barn. Mr. Rutherford had lived there alone since his wife died. He worked in town, coming home in the evenings to care for his three saddlebred mares and a small herd of Black Angus beef cattle.

As Bill continued south along the county road, he imagined the Spook hurling savage expletives at Mr. Rutherford. The climax came when Old Man Crawley pulled a butcher knife, making Mr. Rutherford forget his usual dignity and bolt for his car. That would be a good Spook story to tell Sammy, he mused.

Soon Bill's thoughts returned to the goat his father had denied him. Why wasn't he given a chance? How could he show his folks—especially his pa—that he was old enough to be responsible for an animal of his own when they wouldn't let him have one? If a boy couldn't count on his pa, who could he count on?

An oilcan lay by the edge of the road, and Bill kicked it as he walked. It rattled and banged along the icy gravel so that the sharp sound cut through the gray pall that had closed in around Bill's world.

With a start, he realized that the Cothern farm was only

about half a mile farther. If he continued on, he would miss chores and be late for supper. *So what? Pa thinks I'm irresponsible anyhow*, Bill thought. Over his head last year's oak leaves rattled in the cold wind.

He trudged the rest of the way to the Cothern mailbox, then looked up. The red paint on the barn was fresh, showing off a new sign across its side. Neat white letters spelled out: "Cothern's Goat Dairy," a reminder to Bill that he hadn't seen Mr. Cothern since school started last fall.

Bill walked straight to the kid pen expecting to find Matilda, as usual, with last year's spring does inside the high sheep-fence enclosure. He didn't see her among the others at the far end of the pen, and called. Some of the goats raised their heads, and Bill saw clearly that she was not there. Hearing the clang of a milk pail, he ran toward the barn. "Mr. Cothern," he called, "Where's Matilda?"

A short, plump man with a ready smile on his pink face looked in the direction of the boy's voice. "Her play days are over, sonny. She's bred. Due to kid around the fifteenth of March. She's in the barn with the milkers. You can see her if you like, but I don't want you playing with her anymore." Bill fell into step beside Mr. Cothern, and they walked toward the barn. "Where've you been keeping yourself these days, Billy boy? Haven't seen you in two months of Sundays."

"Chores and school."

They reached the barn; the goats bleated their welcome. "She remembers the hand that feeds her all right." Mr. Cothern put down the milk pail and watched as Matilda trotted over to Bill and pushed her muzzle expectantly into his hand. Bill had come unprepared. The doe nudged his ribs with the curve of her horns to remind him of his neglect. He went to the feed bin to get a handful of grain while Mr. Cothern went about the business of milking. It seemed to Bill that Matilda was a little less slab-

7

sided, but she didn't really show her kid yet. Bill ran his hand over her washboard ribs and the bumps of her hip bones. He had seen brush goats that were fat, but good dairy goats were generally on the thin side with a wide spring to their ribs, like Matilda.

"Save your pennies, and I'll put you down for a kid if she has a doe," Mr. Cothern called across the barn.

"Pa won't let me have one," Bill answered.

"Well, ain't that too bad!" Mr. Cothern exclaimed gaily.

He'd be happy even if Matilda blew away in a hurricane, Bill reflected morosely. Usually he appreciated Mr. Cothern's good-natured gaiety, but tonight it made him feel even more alone. "I'd better be getting home," he said, and started the long walk back.

Bill ran to keep warm. It was not until he drew opposite Mr. Rutherford's barn that he slowed to a walk. Except for his footsteps and his panting, the winter quiet was complete. Suddenly a snort behind him broke into his world, making Bill leap forward, imagining the crawling Spook. A second later, he smiled at his momentary terror. It was, of course, one of the Rutherford horses startled by Bill's running. He went up to the fence and called softly to the mare. The snow squeaked under the hoofs of the approaching animal, and Bill felt the hot breath of the mare on his hand. "Hello, Pheasant. Snuffy tonight, aren't you?" he murmured to the still-snorting mare. "I'd know you by your puffing, even if I couldn't see your blaze."

As he stood at the fence stroking the horse and resting from his run, he noticed that Mr. Rutherford was cleaning out the stable. The light from the door and windows checkered the ground. "Save your pennies," Mr. Cothern had said. An idea began to form in Bill's mind as he watched Mr. Rutherford push the steaming wheelbarrow across the squares of light from the barn. If I bought the kid with my own money... Bill thought. Mr. Rutherford's old for that work. Bill was already running toward him, shouting his name.

"Could I work for you this winter? Could I clean out your barn and feed the horses?"

Bill waited while the old man's eyes traveled slowly from the hood of Bill's parka to his overshoes. It was the same cool search he would give to a mare he considered buying. "Why are you so anxious for the job?"

"I want a kid. A doe. Matilda's going to have one in the spring." Bill realized that it must sound funny for him to predict that Matilda's kid would be a doe. The words had tumbled out before he had time to think them over. Mr. Rutherford did not laugh, and Bill was thankful. "Please." His voice was small in the silence; he wished it had been stronger.

"I believe I'll give you a try. Stop by in the morning, and we'll see what we can work out." He started to pick up his wheelbarrow again, but Bill stepped quickly in front of him and pushed it to the manure pile, dumped it, then returned to the barn. He climbed to the loft, then threw down the straw and hay.

Mr. Rutherford measured out the grain, then leaned against the wall of the box stalls and watched Bill spread the bedding. "Now bring in the horses, Bill." He opened the stall doors, then the barn door. The waiting horses trotted into their stalls and eagerly buried their muzzles in their feed boxes.

The munching and stamping of the horses in the small barn made Bill feel intimate with the proud beasts. His family had failed him, but the horses would help him get Matilda's kid. He wanted to put his face against Pheasant's shoulder, fuzzy with her warm winter coat, and thank her; but Mr. Rutherford was watching. Bill turned away.

"Thank you, Bill. I'll see you in the morning."

Bill took the outstretched hand and responded with a crisp, "Good-bye, sir."

Chapter 2

Jane's Wings

The next morning Bill took time only to gulp milk and grab an apple from the kitchen table as he hurried out the back door to his job. His mother's shouted question, "Billy, where are you going so early?" hung in the air unanswered.

At six thirty he was standing uncertainly midway between Mr. Rutherford's house and barn. Blue, the English setter, barked a greeting to Bill from his kennel. Bill took a few slow steps toward the house. The night before it had been an easy impulse to run up to Mr. Rutherford, but an early morning approach to that forbidding door with the polished brass knocker was harder. *Maybe he likes a guy who just pitches in and does things.* It was easier to walk into the barn than to admit to himself that he was afraid of that door. His stride was longer than usual and there was a purposeful swing to his arms as he entered the barn.

Bill felt an important responsibility as the mares reached their slim heads over their stall doors and nickered. Three pairs of large eyes looked to him for their breakfast. He climbed nimbly to the loft. In a few minutes he had forked timothy down into the mangers, then climbed down the ladder. He was standing, puzzled, in front of two feed drums when a voice behind him caused him to turn.

"Bill, it's a fine thing to get a job done, but it's an even finer thing to find out how to do it first."

"Yes sir," Bill muttered, looking down at a knot in his boot lace.

"Now I'll tell you how we do this, and if you still want the job after you know what it is, it's yours as long as you do it well." Bill followed his new boss around the cleanly swept and white-washed barn and listened to his explanations. "Usually you will lead the horses to the pasture for exercise, but when it's colder than five degrees above zero, I'd like you to leave them in the barn." Bill followed Mr. Rutherford down the feed alley to the last stall. "Pheasant is sensitive to the dust. She has something like an allergy to it."

In confirmation Pheasant sneezed, showering the back of Bill's neck. "Is that like heaves?" he asked. "One of my grandpa's horses got that."

"Yes, that's the usual name for it. To avoid the dust, we wet down her hay after it's in the manger. Ninety percent of the food value is in the leaves, and if we hosed it on the ground, we would lose leaves."

Under close supervision, Bill carried out the cold wet job of pouring water on the hay in Pheasant's manger. As he stood on tiptoes to reach over the bars of the manger, the water and chaff dripped onto his upturned face.

"Now about the grain," continued Mr. Rutherford. "In the left bin is a concentrated horse feed. Melody and Sugar Foot each get three measures of that in the morning. The feed in the right bin is crimped oats with some corn in it, but you don't need to know about that now. Pheasant gets six measures of horse feed. She will foal in the spring, so she needs more feed than the others." Bill followed silently as Mr. Rutherford showed him the rest of the meticulous routine for caring for the registered mares.

Bill was about to go when Mr. Rutherford called him back.

"To begin with, I'll need you only in the mornings. Would fifty cents a day be satisfactory?"

"Yes sir," said Bill. Twice what he had hoped for! Again he turned to go.

"Two things more, and they are most important. First, I don't want you to ride any of the horses under any circumstances. Second, you must never let Blue out of his kennel at any time." Mr. Rutherford held out his hand; Bill shook it, then ran for home. He would have to hurry if he was going to change his boots and make the school bus on time.

* * *

After getting up at five o'clock Bill was tired at school. The day crept to a close. His eyes drifted over the words of his social studies text, but the meaning didn't reach his brain. The girl behind him was blowing her nose; the boy to his left was kicking the legs of his desk. The radiator gurgled, and Bill turned to look through the window above it. His gaze stretched out over the river valley where rich fields lay under white.

He could just make out the peak of the Cothern barn roof where he had walked yesterday. If it were spring he would be able to see the goats, small specks in the pasture nearly two miles away.

In his imagination the snow turned green. Distant fence posts spread out to become a herd of goats, Alpine does with kids moving among them unexpectedly like jumping beans. He saw Matilda leap to him with the swift spring of a deer. As his hands moved up and down his pants leg, he could feel her soft brown coat just as he had the night before, and his knee became the bump of her hip bone. Bill remembered Matilda when she was a little kid dancing on hind legs like black stilts, hoofs against his jeans, trusting as a dog; Matilda with a little grain to coax her, leading like a horse; Matilda coming out of the herd at his call.

Her kid would be his very own. He could make a wagon, paint it red, make a harness with bells. In a flash his kid was a trained goat. He could hear the steady rat-tat-tat of pointy cloven hoofs. Rat-tat-tat. Rat-tat-tat. Louder and louder. Reality snapped his attention to the present. A yellow pencil rapped the edge of his desk. His eyes followed it up a long arm that led to his teacher's face. Bill pulled his feet under his seat, hunched over his book, and squirmed uncomfortably until he heard the teacher clip back to her desk.

★ ★ ★

Standing at his mailbox, Bill watched the orange tail of the school bus roll away, leaving him suspended between school and home. He heard the sound of the engine growing fainter and looked ahead at the snow-packed driveway.

Jane and Sammy chattered to each other in a different world than his. Sammy's back was round with scarves and quilting as he trudged up the hill, Jane's tall and narrow under her straight coat. A year younger than me, and taller, he thought with some bitterness. Jane gave her head a twitch. Like a cat with milk on its whiskers, he thought, watching a red pigtail settle down her back.

As he started up the driveway, Bill noticed Annie, black-and-white from her border collie mom, trotting toward them. She stopped in front of Sammy, then pushed her white-snipped muzzle under the boy's hand. "Thanks for coming to meet me," he said politely as the dog reached an appreciative tongue toward his face. She could just reach Sammy's chin. *What does Annie see in that kid?* Bill kicked a stone into the ditch and watched the fuzzy trail it left in the snow. From the trees in the fencerow to his left a flock of crows was conversing noisily. Bill wished he could understand their calls. It was cold; Bill shrugged, but the cold wouldn't be shaken off. He walked on listening to the crunch his boots made on the packed snow.

By the time he reached the house the yard was deserted. Jane and Sammy had gone inside; Annie had crawled under the porch. The snow in the barnyard was stained and trampled, but the cows were in the barn. The hens were closed in the warm chicken house.

Today Bill was more lonesome than usual. The secret of his new job isolated him, but he wasn't ready to reveal it. Not yet. He could hold on a little longer. Bill leaned against the oak by the back porch and listened for sounds in the January quiet. He was surprised to hear the faint bleat of a goat. Could the sound carry for over a mile? He was sure he heard it. Sound carries far in icy air, he thought, holding his breath in hopes of hearing the plaintive call again. Only winter quiet. Did he imagine Matilda's call?

Bill smiled as he remembered playing with her in the warmth of summer. He missed her. After all, Sammy had Annie, and Jane was always having pets. A goat wouldn't be as much trouble as Jane's squirrel had been. *If I get my own money, Pa just has to let me.* Bill hurried up the back steps and closed the cold behind him.

After the clear air and the sparkle of snow the back porch, with plastic over the screens to block out winter wind, seemed dark and the air heavy with the cow smells that clung to his father's boots and jacket. Bill pulled off his mittens and flung them toward the box on a shelf beside the freezer. They missed the box and fell into the scrub pail. A shadow flew from the corner. Startled, Bill stepped back against the coats hanging from hooks on the other side of the room. "Bats," he gasped. An instant later he knew they couldn't be. Bats would be in hibernation. Suddenly shadows were all about him, fanning his face and teasing his eyes. It was as though the coats had broken into wings and come alive, large wings without bodies jerking through the air. Not bats, not birds. Spirits then? Bill groped for an explanation as he cowered against the wall. He drew his

14

hands behind him, then froze in fear as he felt a light, but clinging, movement on his finger. Slowly he took has hand from behind his back and looked at it. He laughed with relief.

The kitchen door swung open revealing Jane's head. "What's
eating you?" she asked.

"One of your moths, that's what."

"But it couldn't be."

"Oh yes it could. One was creeping up my hand."

Jane leaned forward, tense with dismay, as soft wings
brushcd past hcr hcad. "Oh no!"

Bill wondered why girls always had to get so hysterical about
things.

"What's the matter, dear?" queried Mrs. Brock in her low
voice that was almost always gentle.

"Oh Mom! They've hatched. Hundreds of them, all over.
Who did it?"

Bill watched Jane's pink face screw up, ready for tears. That
was the trouble with redheads. Their faces were always pink.

"I don't know what you mean, dear."

Jane measured her words in a tight voice. "The Cecropias.
Someone took the cocoons out of the freezer, and they've
hatched. Hundreds of them."

"In the first place 'hundreds' couldn't hatch from twenty-five
cocoons, and..."

"Twenty-seven," Jane corrected. "You'll never know how
hard I worked to find all those moth eggs and raise all those
caterpillars."

"All right, twenty-seven. But Jane, I just couldn't leave those
big plastic boxes in the freezer all winter. After your father butchered the pigs, I needed the space. You could have put them outdoors, you know."

"But you didn't *tell* me. Those boxes were the only things I
could find to protect them from squishing. After they froze I

15

could have put them in bags, and they wouldn't have taken hardly any room at all." Jane slumped, limp as she watched the moths flutter into corners. "They wouldn't stay at a nice even temperature outdoors."

"Jane, you aren't being sensible. Do you think wild moths have houses equipped with deep freezes?"

"Oh Mom, but why couldn't you just *tell* me?"

"I didn't think of it."

"Aw, quit griping and get your butterfly net," Bill said.

"Billy's right. The moths are all over the kitchen. In a few minutes they'll be in the soup."

"But do you realize what this means? I can't breed them *now*, in the middle of *winter*. I couldn't get anything for the caterpillars to eat. I'll have to catch wild ones next summer and start *all over*."

"Feed 'em parsley," Sammy suggested. "Ma's got it in pots."

"Don't be ridiculous. Black swallowtail larvae eat parsley. Cecropias eat lilac and trees and stuff like that. Stuff I can't get in the winter."

"Aw, Jane, calm down." Bill looked around the kitchen, bright with yellow walls, fluttering with large-winged moths.

"It's my whole next year's income."

"Miss Sorenson doesn't want to buy hundreds," Bill noted. "There just aren't that many kids in her biology class."

"She said she wanted all I could raise."

"She wouldn't have if she'd known how many you'd get."

"Will you shut up!" Jane spat out the words.

"Children. That's enough. Jane, get your net." Mrs. Brock's tone left no room for disobedience. Jane started toward the back porch. "Not there. I put it in your closet."

Mrs. Brock shook her head and smiled as her daughter went upstairs. "If I weren't trying to get dinner in the middle of all this, it would seem funny."

"What?" asked Bill.

"I wasn't talking to anyone in particular."

Bill was ready for his turn to be noticed. "Say, Mom, know what?"

"I can't read your mind. Just tell me."

"I heard a goat bleating when I came home from school —almost sure," he added doubtfully.

"Did you? Jane, do hurry." Mrs. Brock started to brush a moth off the bread board, then backed away as she saw Jane coming through the door with her net.

"You know what I've been thinking?" Bill continued.

Jane was beside the table; Mrs. Brock turned her attention away from Bill. "Come catch this moth so I can slice some bread."

"Isn't she beautiful?" Jane held out her hand, and the moth quivered its feathered antennae and placed one red-velvet leg on Jane's finger. The rose-and-tawny wings, with their light eye-spots, raised slightly as the moth clung to Jane's finger. "I have to kill you," she said softly, "But freezing doesn't hurt much."

"Yeah, a swell way to die. Can I be next?" Bill snorted.

Jane ignored her brother. "Ma, can I have some jars?"

Mrs. Brock went to the shelf and returned with a stack of plastic freezing cartons. "Here you go." Bill watched as Jane put her finger in the carton and with the other hand held the cover ready. She slid her finger from the carton without allowing the moth to escape and put it into the freezer. Bill was glad he couldn't see the wing beats slow, then quiver and stop. To him death was scary, even if it was just a moth freezing.

The other moths followed, but not all as easily as the first. The afternoon wore on. Supper was almost ready. The table was set. The milk was poured. Two moths still fluttered around the ceiling light.

"How you gonna get 'em?" Sammy wanted to know.

"Easy." Jane stepped onto the table just as the outside door opened. Bill turned to look.

The kitchen door framed his father. His slim body, wind-red face, and sandy hair brought their wrapping of cold air into the room. His blue eyes shone with the hard sparkle of a winter sky. "What are you doing on the table?!" he exclaimed.

In answer Jane gave her net an enthusiastic swipe, and the light bulb shattered all over the kitchen. Glass rained into the milk and formed a mosaic on the butter. Jane bolted from the room in tears, leaving the two moths fluttering in the net.

"What the?..." Mr. Brock muttered in confusion. His wife came up from the basement with a quart of applesauce and began to explain the situation. "Jane's all upset because I..."

Bill didn't listen. Just like Jane, he was thinking—gets everything all stirred up and then ducks out. In the confusion of broken glass and tumbled furniture, Bill noticed the net lying on the floor shaking like a ghost in a bear trap. "After all the trouble she takes to raise them, you'd think she'd at least keep them from battering themselves ragged," he mumbled, picking up the net with a sweep and a twist that trapped the moths in the top of the deep bag. He took the net outside and leaned it against the rail of the back porch, then came back into the kitchen feeling as though he had just stepped from a cold shower.

Jane was back in the kitchen. "Who stole my butterfly net?" Her accusing eyes pranced from one face to another, then settled on Bill's.

"Stream's still open. Thought I'd use it to net some minnows," he teased.

"Give it to me. It had two moths in it."

Bill shrugged his shoulders and moved away. Mrs. Brock pushed a broom into Jane's hands. "Sweep up the glass, Jane. Billy, you move the chairs for your sister, and no more teasing."

"But where's my net?"

"I put it out on the back porch. The moths'll freeze quick out there."

The kitchen had been restored to order, and Mrs. Brock was pouring fresh milk. "What's burning?" Mr. Brock asked, sniffing.

"Oh, the beans!" exclaimed his wife. Sammy rushed to the stove, turned the wrong control, reached across the stove to take off the beans, and singed his shirtsleeve on the burner he had just turned on. His mother got there in time to rescue Sammy, but not the beans.

They said grace as usual, led in Mr. Brock's deep voice. Stability was restored, and the meal was finished quietly.

After supper Mr. Brock pushed back his chair. "Going out to the barn," he said, walking toward the door. He smiled. "Cows are a lot more peaceful."

Bill ran after him. "Know what I've been thinking about doing?"

"I know what you should be thinking about doing. Your books are on the chair. Take them upstairs, and *do it now*. Dreams won't get you anywhere."

As the door closed behind his father, Bill thought about dreams. For him it took a good strong dream to start the action. It was like a motor to make things happen. But his father didn't see it that way. Maybe better to keep his plan to himself. It wouldn't do to risk another "No."

One corner of his room was filled by a dark rolltop desk that had belonged to his grandfather. Bill pulled his chair up to it and started his arithmetic. There was a lot, twenty-five problems. He headed his paper and read the directions.

When he finally finished his arithmetic, Bill was ready for bed and lost no time sliding under the covers. Good, he thought as his mother's soft tread approached his door. When she comes to say good night, I'll say something about Matilda's kid—just a little to feel her out.

She had just stepped inside his room when Jane wailed out, "Oh, no. This is the *worst!*" His mother kissed him quickly, then went to Jane. Bill could hear every word. "It broke off," she was saying, "the whole wing, and it was an absolutely perfect specimen."

"Jane, I told you not to do any mounting tonight. There's been enough fuss over those moths for one day."

"But I just had to spread the ones Bill left in the net. A wind or something might have blown them off the porch and wrecked them up."

His mother's voice became inaudible, then rose again as she asked Jane, "Did you brush your teeth?"

"I was just going to."

"Hurry then, and get back to bed." His mother went downstairs.

Bill turned on his side, hugging his pillow to him. "Too soft," he muttered. A goat would feel hard and angular and smell of fresh hay. His parents would let him have it, sure, but maybe... The doubtful thought troubled him. Restless, he got up to get a glass of water.

As he stepped into the hall, he saw the flutter of Jane's nightgown and caught the light on the kinks of her unbraided hair as she returned to her room. Bill stopped at the partially opened door and watched her dash halfway across the room, then leap for her bed. She dived under the covers like a frightened chick to the old cluck's wing.

"What are you doing anyway? Practicing for a broad jump?"

"I didn't know you were there. I always get into bed that way." She drew in a breath as though about to say more, then hesitated.

"You act like the Spook was chasing you or something."

"Oh, don't be silly. I'm not scared of Mr. Crawley. He's just a neighbor I know, even if he is kind of spooky-strange. I just..."

She broke off. "It's kind of hard to say. Promise you won't tell?" He nodded. She opened and closed her mouth a few times before revealing herself. "When it's dark and everything it's like something spooky was waiting under the bed to catch my feet. Course I know it's really okay, but still..."

"So you invent something to be afraid of?"

"Oh, shh. In the summer it isn't so bad, last summer I mean. There were all the caterpillars, and when I was real still I could hear them munching their leaves, and it was kind of comforting."

Bill laughed. "That's a good one. A bunch of worms to comfort you."

"You don't even *try* to understand."

Their mother's voice floated up the stairs. "Children, settle down."

Bill got his glass of water, then went back to bed wishing he hadn't been quite so hard on Jane. He turned toward the window. It was quiet out there. Even the dry leaves on the oaks had ceased their rustling. He missed the sound.

Chapter 3

No Bed of Roses

The cold night lingered into the morning as Bill stepped from the light of the horse barn and started to walk toward home. The icy air filling his lungs chilled him from the inside out. For the second day Bill needed to hurry home from work, grab something to eat—if there was time—then change his barn boots for school shoes and overshoes and run for the bus.

The chores had gone smoothly, everything the same as before except that Mr. Rutherford had put a small ladder next to Pheasant's manger so that Bill would not have to lift the dripping hay over his head. He left the barn thinking everything was turning out neat. But he did feel uneasy about his secret. *Pa'd soon have to know*. He'd skipped out on milking when he got so mad about the kid. Then last night he was real tired, and when he made it to the barn, his pa already had the cows cleaned. The milking machine sat on the floor, and his pa was fitting it on the last cow. Bill shrugged it off. He wasn't going to quit his job. That was for sure.

As Bill approached the Crawley place there was no room in his mind for fearful thoughts about the Spook, but he did notice the streams of light coming through the cracks in the door, so he knew that Crawley was milking. While he watched, a square of light appeared in the corral between the barn and the road, and a cow darkened the door and raced toward Bill. The Spook followed, a grotesque figure flapping in the half-light. Above his head he held his homemade milk stool, a piece of one-by-ten nailed on top of a short log. He was swearing at the skinny cow as he raced behind her. He cornered the terrified beast only a few feet from the road where Bill stood.

"Kick me into the gutter, will you," he snarled, flailing the bawling creature with the stool until she pushed down a rotten post and plunged through the fence into the ditch beside the road. As Crawley wove his way back to the barn, Bill could see, even in the early morning half-light, that his clothes were as foul as his speech.

Bill easily reconstructed the events leading to the scene he had watched. The one-legged milk stool made Crawley's seat precarious. A sudden movement by the cow must have sent him sprawling into the gutter, milk and manure drenching him from head to foot. This would be something worth telling Jane and Sammy while they waited for the bus.

"Who's that?" The Spook's voice. Crawley after his cow. Bill should have expected it. He raced toward home, his boots pounding the snow-packed gravel. Crawley could never catch him; Bill knew it. He reached his house in minutes and bounded up the porch steps two at a time. In the back room, he kicked his barn boots into the corner and pulled on his school shoes and overshoes.

The inviting smell of coffee and bacon wafted from the kitchen door, and he was glad there was time to grab a slice of bacon before hurrying down to the bus.

★ ★ ★

When five o'clock came, Bill was again late for chores. He had fallen asleep on the living room couch and missed his pa's call for milking. He didn't wake up until after dinnertime. Sammy and Jane had left the table; his parents were finishing their pie when Bill slid into his place.

"Where have you been?" his father questioned sternly. "You know I need your help with milking."

"Busy," Bill answered through a mouthful of cold pork.

"Billy, don't talk with your mouth full," his mother admonished.

His father, unsatisfied, continued the inquisition. "What were you doing?"

Bill's mouth was still full. Telling his pa how tired he was would lead to questions about why. He needed to guard his new life from his parents, especially now when his job felt so new and fragile. He let the question go unanswered. Bill watched nervously as his father finished his coffee, took a toothpick from the center of the table, pushed his chair back, then left the room chewing the end of the toothpick. This time he had been lucky.

Bill slathered a piece of fresh bread in cold gravy and ate it with relish. His mother was washing dishes. Her blond hair gleamed in the light from the bulb above the sink. "This sure is good, Ma!" he exclaimed.

"If you kept it in your mouth long enough to taste it, I'd call that quite a compliment," she retorted, smiling as she scraped the plates.

Bill gave a muffled snicker. If he opened his mouth to laugh, he'd lose the good food that filled it. For the rest of the meal, he gave all his attention to eating. After shoveling in the last bite of his second helping of pie, Bill scraped his chair back with a contented sigh. "You sure are some cook."

"That sounds nice, but you wouldn't know the difference if I gave you raw pork when you're hungry as you were tonight."

Raw pork. The words reminded him of the dead sow, and

Old Man Crawley cast an unpleasant foreboding across his happiness.

"Why is Mr. Crawley the way he is?" Bill asked abruptly.

"I don't know just how to answer that. What way do you mean?"

Bill carried his plate to the sink as he thought. "Dirty and mean to everybody, and to his stock, too," he added, remembering the crack of the milk stool on the cow's hip bone. "And living all alone without any friends at all. Doug said he looked in the kitchen window once, and there was garbage and old papers on the floor so he couldn't even see the boards."

"Well," his mother said slowly, "People were never meant to live alone." She paused.

"Why does he do it then? Cows are dumb, but you never see a cow live away from a herd unless somebody makes her—or when she's calving." Crawley didn't fit into anything he knew about the world. It bothered him.

"When Mr. Crawley was a little boy, his father came here from the old country," his mother began, "and they didn't even speak our language."

"What about his mother?"

"She died when Mr. Crawley was very young. His father worked hard, but he didn't know how to farm. He had been a miner, and he farmed the same way he went after coal. Just threw the manure into the stream to get rid of it and took crops off the land without ever fertilizing it."

"Didn't anyone tell him not to?"

"Your grandfather Brock tried to tell him, but he wouldn't listen to anyone. I think he was ashamed of not knowing the language. Your father told me what he said. 'We got our own way.' Farming a hundred and twenty acres is hard work, and he died young. All he left his son was a worn-out farm and false ideas on how to farm it."

"You mean he hates everybody because he's a poor farmer?"

"No, not exactly. But to be a good farmer, you have to love your land and love your stock. You need to be generous to your stock and to the soil that feeds them. You have to help your neighbor, give as well as take. And you need the same qualities if you are going to live happily with people."

Bill watched his mother's hands disappear under the suds in the dishpan. "I sort of get it, I guess. But it's kind of freaky." Bill was reminded again of the two-headed pig fetus he had seen in the Hudson grain elevator. "He's sort of a freak in the head then, isn't he?"

"That's one way of putting it." His mother had nearly finished with the dishes that were piled beside the sink. "Call Jane to dry the dishes. Tell Sammy not to start another program. He's been glued to the radio long enough."

Bill walked into the living room and abruptly terminated the sound of galloping horses. "Ma says you can't listen to any more radio."

"Bill!" It was his mother's voice from the kitchen. "I said he couldn't start *another* program."

Sammy quickly turned the program back on and listened to the gunfire terminating the cattle rustler just in time to save the sheriff's little brother from his clutches.

"Hey, Jane," Bill bellowed.

"Don't shout. Go upstairs and find her. She's probably mounting moths."

"I don't have to. Here she is." Jane went into the kitchen, and Bill joined Sammy to hear the end of the program.

"I've got a good one on the Spook," he said when the commercial came on.

"Okay. Tell it to me while I get ready for bed."

Bill went upstairs with his brother and told him about the sow in the road. "And it had two heads," he finished.

"You're kidding."

Bill thought hard about the wrinkled creature in the jar of formaldehyde. "No, honest, hope to die. It had two heads." Next he told about the noise he had heard when he passed the Crawley place. He embellished it, telling Sammy how he had crept close and heard what the Spook said, then saw him pull a knife. Sammy's eyes were wide and fearful. Then came the comedy relief. "You should have seen him! Just sopped with stinking manure."

His mother came to kiss Sammy good night. Bill told her about the cow kicking Crawley and the beating. "Poor thing," his mother murmured. "People like that shouldn't be allowed to have livestock. Time for prayers now," she said more cheerfully.

Bill went to his own room and closed the door. He wanted to do some figuring before he saw Mr. Rutherford Friday morning, so he went to his desk to get paper and pencil. He tried to open the top, but it was pulled down and locked. The key should be in the middle drawer, but when he tried that, he found that it was locked too. After searching in several unlocked drawers, he found the key under his socks. "Ten dollars," he muttered, finding a pencil and a Sear's order blank to figure on. "Nearly two months until March fifteenth. That's about sixty days. Fifty cents a day, that would be...thirty dollars. That leaves me twenty dollars for a chain and feed and even enough to start saving for a cart." Bill pushed the paper to the back of his desk, relieved and happy.

Feeling confident that the unborn kid was as good as his, he pulled open the file drawer of his desk. In it was a mass of leather harness straps tied together with string and baling twine. As he looked at the tangle, he felt discouraged. It would take a lot of doing to make that stuff into a respectable goat harness. The leather needed a good soaping, and the string ties looked pretty bad. Then he remembered the plastic lacing thread in some other drawer. After looking through several, he found it: red, orange, blue, and green. The colors were tangled together. Pretty late to start the harness now, and I've got to get up real early tomorrow, Bill mused. With a yawn he pushed the straps and laces to the back of the desk and rolled down the top.

As he was getting ready for bed, Bill heard the voices of his parents coming from the register in the floor by the foot of his bed. Usually their conversation wasn't worth listening to. At first he didn't pay much attention, but on the way back from brushing his teeth, he heard his name float up on the warm air rising through the grillwork. This might be interesting. He pulled back the rag rug that covered most of the grill, took the feather comforter from his bed, and curled up comfortably, his ear to the current of warmth and sound from the living room. "...just asked me to give it to him," his father was saying, "and if I had, he'd be asking you to take care of it for him. That's the trouble with the whole country. Kids don't know what work is, just ask for handouts, and their parents go begging to the government. We've got a great country here, if we just don't go and spoil it by pulling the backbone out of our kids."

"I believe Billy has plenty of backbone," Martha Brock said softly.

George Brock was warming to his subject, and his wife's quiet confidence went unnoticed. "Why even the stock's getting soft. You can't raise a heifer without half a dozen kinds of medicine, and they're even rigging up shower baths for pigs. Now that tribe in Africa..."

"You mean the one that keeps for breeding the calves that get up and walk the soonest?"

"Yeah, did I tell you that before?" George went on without waiting for an answer. "Anyhow, Billy's not going to have the backbone taken out of him if I can help it..."

"And what was it your father said when he came over from

Germany?" Martha broke in. "'My boy isn't going to have to slave the way I did to make ends meet.' That was it, wasn't it?"

"Yeah, but I was lucky. He couldn't afford to spoil me. He did see that I got a college education though, and I'll do the same for Billy...if he'll work for part of it."

"Well, dear, I think you'd better just give away the tractor and milking machine and really make a man out of him."

"That would be better than going out to the barn and pushing buttons to feed the cattle the way Cummings does. Kim, that boy of his, never does a lick of work, and look at him, soft as one of those sultans sitting on a cushion all day."

"Remember, Billy's only twelve, and all he did was ask you to let him have a goat. Jane has pets."

"She gets them for herself, and she takes care of them herself. But that Billy—Tuesday and again tonight he didn't show for milking, and yesterday he was late and half asleep on his feet. I suppose he's hiding out after school with that friend of his."

"You mean Doug Mason? What with his parents both gone all day I'm glad he has Billy next door. I like him. He's a nice energetic boy in spite of his parents' neglect."

Something under the comforter was poking Bill in the ribs, and he rolled to one side.

"I still think I'm right. Billy's going to work every inch of the way. He'll get no coddling from me." The pricking continued, and Bill groped in the folds of the comforter as his father went on. "If I treated him like a lot of the parents I know, he'd be as soft as those Sybarites that slept on beds of roses and yelled if there were any crumpled petals..." George broke off suddenly as a small piece of baling wire clattered down through the register.

"Apparently there are some thorns among Billy's rose petals," Martha said crisply as she stooped to pick up the bit of wire.

Pa always talking about work—like a boy couldn't grow up without practically killing himself with it. Why does everything have to be so hard? Bill wondered as he slid between the sheets, with anger at his father, almost, but not quite strong enough to keep him awake.

I'll show him, was his last thought before falling asleep.

Chapter 4

The Fall

Friday. Bill hurried to Mr. Rutherford's, thankful that the weather had warmed to twenty above, so he could hay the horses in the pasture. All he would have to do is fluff the hay in the snow. But he would have to lead the mares, one at a time, across the driveway to the pasture gate beyond the garage.

On this, his third day, Bill was entirely alone. He heard the impatient Pheasant striking at her stall door as he measured out the grain.

With feed boxes full, the sounds changed to contented munching. Bill headed for the ladder to the loft for hay and more bedding straw. To open a new bale of straw, he needed the pliers for cutting baling wire. It should be hanging on a nail in the stud. It was gone. He planned to hunt for it after he took care of the barn. He let the mares into the paddock while he took out the manure, then loaded the hay into the cart and wheeled it to the pasture. All this was taking longer than he had expected, but it would never do to lose the cutting pliers. He hurried back up the ladder to hunt for it. The longer he groped in the straw that covered the floor of the loft, the more determined he became in his search. The dim light of the loft slowed Bill's sense of time. His gloved hands continued to rake the straw until a spray of light

31

found a knothole in the east wall of the barn, showing Bill how late it was getting. He pushed down a bale of straw, hoping it would burst open when it fell, but it held its shape like an enormous yellow brick. He went down the ladder into the feed room. His fingers were freezing as he struggled to pull the bedding from the tightly wired bale. All he could do was pull it out, stem by stem. He straightened up, defeated. As he started for the door, a glint at his feet caught his eye. The pliers! He must have pushed it down with the hay. Hurriedly, he clipped the wire. It took only a few minutes to bed the stalls, then he was leading Melody and Sugar Foot from the paddock to the pasture.

As he snapped the lead rope to Pheasant's halter, it occurred to him that he would have a much better chance of making that bus if he could ride to the end of the pasture. He remembered how easy it was to ride old Nell, his grandfather's retired draft horse.

Bill led Pheasant through the pasture gate, her caulked shoes striking the frozen ground with clean beats. The mare stood quietly against the white rail fence while Bill latched the gate. As he reached to unsnap the lead rope from her halter, she obligingly lowered her head and pushed her muzzle against his neck. *Just this once...* Instead of unsnapping the rope, he knotted the free end to the halter ring, improvising a pair of reins. He stepped to the bottom rail of the fence, flung the loop over the mare's head, and climbed to the top rail. It was a simple matter to settle down easily to the mare's back. Pheasant picked up her head, then gave it a toss in a puzzled effort to find the bit. Bill clamped his legs to her sides as he felt her muscles tense under her soft winter coat. The light touch of Bill's heels was cue enough for the sensitive Pheasant. Her muscles uncoiled in a high canter. The slight weight on her back rose and fell first to one side, then to the other. Pheasant grew nervous under the strange unbalanced load she carried. As she went into a small gully, she once more

32

stretched out her head in an attempt to find the accustomed support of the bit. Finding no restraint but the strange jerking pull on her halter, she speeded up the other side of the gully. Bill slipped back and fell clumsily over her kidneys. The mare's confusion turned to terror, and she forgot her careful schooling. Without the meticulous control she was used to, Pheasant's great energy exploded in speed. It was as though she reverted to the days of wild horses when a weight on a horse's back meant a predator leaping for the kill. Bill gripped the makeshift reins with one hand and Pheasant's mane with the other. His supple body flexed with the powerful strides of the horse. Somehow he retained his seat. As the ground flew under him, he made a desperate effort to calm the flying horse. "Easy, gal," he soothed. The slow, comforting words were lost in the wind, and the horse raced on toward her stable mates, now at the far end of the pasture. Bill held his breath as the fence rushed towards him. Fear tensed his muscles as his mount continued her breakneck pace. It was impossible for Bill to grip those hard undulating sides, and he relied on balance alone. If he was going to stay on her back, he had to know what she would do when she came to the fence. At that speed, she could not possibly turn, he thought. She will have to jump. He reckoned without a knowledge of his horse. Pheasant was a five-gaited mare, and she had never jumped under saddle. She wanted to gain the security of her stable mates and would make no attempt to sail the fence she had respected all her life. She wheeled to the left, and Bill was flung violently against the fence post.

He lay against the frozen ground. Snow was in his mouth. He licked his lips and tasted blood, but he couldn't tell where it came from. Nothing hurt.

The school bus. He'd have to hurry to make it. He pulled his left leg under him. As he did so, a paralyzing pain shot through his right leg. Bill looked back over his right shoulder. He saw first a thin trickle of blood across the snow. His foot was strangely twisted. As he lay there, face down in the snow, breathing in gasps, the realization came to him slowly. *Broken.*

Unless he could get to the road, no one would find him. Experimentally he moved his shoulders. His arms were all right, so was his left leg. The road stretched in front of him, only about fifteen feet away, but looking as inaccessible as a distant mountain range. He stretched his left arm forward and grabbed a fence post. With the help of his left leg and right arm, he dragged himself forward toward the fence. Pain beat through him and made him cry aloud. Inch by inch he crawled and dragged himself along. Once under the fence, poplars and box elders offered handholds allowing him, painfully, to pull himself toward the road. Could he make the final rise to the shoulder? There were no trees to help him there, and the packed snow was slippery. He pushed forward with his left leg, clutched a stalk of sumac, and pulled himself a few more inches. He reached up to the shoulder of the road; his foot found support on the sumac. He gave one final shove. As he did so, he cried out in pain and despair. The laces of his right boot had snagged on some brush, trapping his injured leg.

He rubbed his face into the snow and clutched at dead grass with his hands. As he lay there, moaning softly, he felt rather than heard the rumble of a heavy vehicle on the road. *They won't see me.* His thoughts tormented him. He raised his left arm to wave. As he held it there, he heard the wheels pass him, squeal to a stop, then back up. He heard steps crossing the highway. In relief he let his exhausted arm fall back.

"Bill, is that you? What happened?" It was Mr. Erickson, the bus driver. Bill was glad it was no stranger. He liked Mr. Erickson.

"It's my leg," he answered. Mr. Erickson needed to ask no more—the prints of the galloping horse, the turf thrown up on the snow where the horse had turned, the shred of denim snagged on the fence post, and finally the drag marks flecked with blood.

Mr. Erickson turned toward the bus. "Mark, come here," he called. A tall Eagle Scout of about sixteen stepped down from the bus and crossed the road, shortly followed by other curious passengers. "Get back in that bus, kids."

"Me too?" Jane asked.

"Yes, all of you. I asked for Mark." The children returned to the bus, and Mr. Erickson turned to Mark. "His right leg may be broken. Looks like a compound fracture, so we'd best splint it here. I'll drive back and tell his folks." The driver took off his coat and spread it over Bill.

Mark, who was kneeling beside Bill, looked up at Mr. Erickson. "Send Doug out to help me, will you? And get a knife. We'll have to cut splints."

To Bill this conversation seemed to come from another world. He had reached the road; his job was over. Now he was in the hands of his friends.

In a few seconds Bill heard the bus drive off. Then Doug joined Mark, calling as he came, "I got a good sharp knife and a bunch of scarves to bind the splint on with."

"Good," said Mark. He looked at Bill and grinned. "I'd have hated to tear up a good shirt for that sad looking bag of bones."

Bill forced a smile. "Thanks," he said.

The boys worked quickly, and Bill managed to keep back the tears, although not the groans of pain. By the time Mr. Brock drove up, Mark and Doug had the leg splinted. His father had brought blankets and an old army cot that worked fine as a stretcher. It hurt plenty when they moved him, but it was nothing like the pain he had felt when he was crawling.

Once propped up in the back seat of the car, Bill realized

what his injury would mean, and the thought of losing his kid was more painful to him than his leg.

"What in blazes were you doing on Mr. Rutherford's horse?" his father demanded after a long restrained silence.

The question tore into his already painful thoughts, and sobs choked his reply. "I was trying to catch the school bus."

"But why..." his father began, then broke off as he realized that it was asking too much to expect Bill to talk.

A shred of hope: perhaps he could go back to work in a month. Then he would have a month to work before Matilda would kid in March—if Mr. Rutherford would take him back.

Bill was afraid to ask his father, but he couldn't stand not knowing. Finally, just as they were approaching the hospital, the question came: "How long does it take a broken leg to heal?"

"Eight or ten weeks, I guess, but I don't know for sure."

Eight or ten weeks! All Bill's hopes and careful plans were shattered by his father's words. Who would help him now that he couldn't help himself? *Not my pa*, Bill thought.

Chapter 5

A Kid Is Born

Bill was wheeled from the emergency dressing room to the X-ray room, back to the dressing room, then to the operating room. Words passed through the air with foreign sounds: "radius okay," "oblique fracture," "tibia," "compound." Bill floated away from the words around him: A goat bleated in the distance, loud plaintive cries. Bill tried to follow. The bleating faded, and he couldn't move his legs to follow it. He cried, it hurt, and he woke up. The doctors were gone.

"What were you dreaming?" It was his mother's comfortable voice.

"I couldn't catch my goat," he murmured, still half in his dream.

"Next year, darling. You'll be able to get it then."

"Next year! This one's just starting!" Bill turned his face to the wall. He lay helpless on the bed. The past was over, the future empty.

"I brought a book to read to you." Bill made no comment. He didn't care if his mother stayed or went. But she opened the cover, and her voice rolled on, waves beating in pleasant monotony. A nurse passed through; his lunch tray came and went.

"I have to go now." His mother stood up. "The doctor thinks

37

you can come home tomorrow morning," she said cheerfully, then kissed him and left.

The next morning Bill received an envelope bearing Mr. Rutherford's return address. It contained a check for $1.50 and a terse note: "Dear Bill: I am sorry you had to learn the hard way that there are reasons for the instructions I give. Your job will be waiting for you when your leg is mended. Sincerely yours, R. H. Rutherford."

"Nice of him," Bill thought, but with no chance to buy the kid, he didn't feel much pleasure.

Soon after Bill had read the note, his father came to take him home. "How's the old leg this morning?" George Brock's voice was kinder than usual.

"Okay, I guess."

"The doctor been in yet?"

"No."

"We'd better wait for him." After an awkward silence he went on, "You know, I was pleased that you got that job for yourself."

Bill listened flatly. His father's praise was a rare thing, and ordinarily he valued it, but today he valued nothing.

George Brock cleared his throat and said, "It's a serious thing to disobey instructions when you hold a responsible job."

A nurse's soft shoes were stepping in the hall, followed by the brisk tread of the doctor.

"Hello there, young fellow. You certainly took quite a spill." The doctor turned to Bill's father, but the boy didn't listen. As he was going, he spoke to Bill again. "What we have here is an oblique fracture." He put his two fists together. "Now this is what will happen if you're too rough on that leg," he explained as he slid his fists apart. "We've got a good set, and we want to keep it that way. *No weight on that cast.* You'll get a walking cast in about seven weeks."

"Seven weeks before I can walk!" Bill exclaimed.

"You're lucky. It would be longer than that if you'd broken both bones. Now don't get smart with those crutches. Stay inside when it's icy." Over his shoulder, as he hurried out, "Get your dad to give you one of those pills I gave him if the pain gets too rough."

Bill went home. Even Jane was nice to him at first. She brought him his tray and rubbed his itching toes. She meant well, but whenever she rubbed hard enough to keep from tickling, it hurt. "Okay," she said, "I don't want to rub your stinky toes anyway."

Jane left the room. Bill turned to his mother who was washing the window. "Why does she always have to say something mean?"

Mrs. Brock rubbed the lint from the corner of a pane before answering. "Jane gets her feelings hurt easily..."

"I don't think she has any."

"If she didn't, she wouldn't try to cover them up with sharp remarks. Remember, she was trying to make you feel better, and you told her she was hurting—made her feel worse than useless."

"What was I supposed to do? Let her twist my foot off?"

Mrs. Brock had finished the window. "My words aren't getting through to you. Some day you'll just have to find out for yourself that you can't get along with people until you forget yourself and try to understand them." With impatient speed, his mother gathered up her rags and left the room.

Hobbling around on crutches was no substitute for two good legs. A January thaw followed by zero temperatures made for ice-covered ground, so Bill's mother drove him to and from the school bus. At home he spent most of his time inside. Although he could slide down the banister, going upstairs on one crutch and gripping the banister with the other hand was slow going.

The dull ache in his right leg was replaced by itching he couldn't scratch, and people soon stopped trying to bolster his morale by talking about how brave he was to have crawled to the road. The days slid by him like snails across a turtle's shell.

January passed and February followed. Bill spent a good deal of his time stretched on his bed reading or doing homework. His trapped muscles furiously demanded activity, but he still couldn't step on his bad leg. The slow days had given Bill much time to grieve over his lost opportunity to earn his kid, and he had become so sullen that the other members of the family would hardly speak to him.

★ ★ ★

On a Saturday in early March, Bill sprawled on his bed watching drops fall from the tip of an icicle hanging from the eaves outside his window. The cardinals and chickadees, too, had noticed the breaking of winter, and the males were beginning to sing out their territorial claims. The feeder that his mother kept filled was fluttering with hollow-boned fliers, and Bill watched them with interest. A chickadee fluffed its feathers in the snow, then rose as easily as a gas-filled balloon and paused in the air just outside Bill's window to drink a drop from the icicle. Eagerly Bill called his mother, but she came too late. The acrobatic chickadee had quenched its thirst and gone. Now a squirrel scampered across the yard and up the trunk of the oak tree as though it were level ground. Bill envied it. "For him it's so easy to move."

"Soon it will be for you. Remember? You get your walking cast next Monday," she said as she left the room.

★ ★ ★

It was his second day in the walking cast. The sun had begun to honeycomb the snow, and Bill was restless as the March wind.

"Ma, what's the date?"

"The sixteenth of March. Why?"

Bill caught his breath; Matilda could have her kid by now. She was due yesterday. To his mother he said casually, "Just curious. Okay if I go out?"

"I suppose. If you're careful to keep your cast dry."

Bill's mother helped him put on his left boot and solved the problem of keeping his cast dry by wrapping his right foot in plastic freezer bags.

With the help of his cane, Bill clumped down the wooden steps, looked over his shoulder to make sure no one was watching him, then started toward the county road. The two-hundred-yard driveway used to seem no distance at all to Bill, who ran more than he walked. Now he pushed forward against the restraints of his heavy cast and weak muscles. When, finally, he reached the mailbox, he began to doubt that he ever would get to the Cotherns'. What could he do when he got there? All that way just to tell Matilda that he couldn't have her kid? It didn't make sense, but he wanted to see her. In his determination, Bill kept his eyes to the gravel ahead of him and plodded on. There was a dull ache in his right leg, and his left leg was tired before he had gone halfway.

The Cothern farm seemed to Bill as inaccessible as the moon. But slowly the road passed under his feet, the endless distance became yards, the yards feet, and finally Bill was standing at the barn door. He opened it and left the bright light of sky and snow.

Mr. Cothern greeted him. "I see you're using the old peg again. Good enough. Say, looks like you and the stork are getting here together."

"Where's Matilda?" Bill couldn't see her with the other does.

"She's in the kidding pen in the corner." Mr. Cothern pointed with his manure fork. "Since this is her first kid, it

41

would be a good idea if you kept an eye on her. I'd like to finish cleaning the place out. That okay with you?"

"Sure. I've helped Pa with calves lots of times." He had assisted his father only once, but it was important to him to gain Mr. Cothern's respect

"Goats aren't so different. More high-strung though. Matilda'll probably do all right by herself, but there can always be problems. Remember, feet first. Through the sack you'll see the lead hoof with a nice soft cartilage cap, then the other foot, and the head tucked between the front legs. When you see that little nose, you're home free. If anything else happens, there's trouble, and you call me quick."

Bill listened carefully then nodded, glad Mr. Cothern had briefed him. He hooked his cane over the wall of the kidding pen and went inside. The small space was lit by two windows, one on either side of the corner. Matilda was flicking her tail, a quick agitation. Bill noticed a gelatinous discharge and saw that the young doe's udder had filled. When she saw him, Matilda got up and trotted to the boy, bleating softly. Her eyes were bright, her step quick, and the kid inside had bulged out her ribs.

"You're gonna be a mom pretty soon, Kid." Bill checked her swollen udder. It was hard and shiny, so Bill gently squeezed out a little of the milk. One of the barn cats came up with an open mouth ready to receive the thin stream. The kidding pen had not yet been cleaned, and Bill, wanting to find a fork, turned too quickly, then cringed with the pain as he attempted to catch his weight on his broken leg. Holding on to the side of the pen, he hopped to the fork he saw leaning against the wall near the gate he had entered. He worked slowly, and the pain in his broken leg eased. When he had piled the manure outside the pen, he went to the feed room and brought an armload of clean straw that he spread with the fork. As he worked, Matilda's nervousness increased. She lay down, got up, and lay down again in quick succession. Bill finished spreading the last of the straw and reached out the door to lean the fork against the wall outside the pen so that there would be no chance of Matilda's injuring herself on the prongs. A sharp, crying bleat spun Bill around. There was a throb of pain in his leg, but he gave it only passing notice. As the doe cried, she threw her hindquarters against the wall of the pen. Bill took her by a horn with one hand, and with the other he stroked her neck. "Easy, girl, it won't be long now." Even as he spoke, the doe bleated again and spun her hindquarters from one side to the other. She hated being held by her horn, but Bill couldn't restrain her any other way. He was afraid she might injure the kid if she threw herself against the walls of the pen. He ran his hand over her well-sprung ribs, feeling contractions in the tight abdominal walls. Matilda's bleating was almost continuous now as she swung her body from side to side while Bill gripped her left horn. "Don't be such a cry-baby," he admonished gently. Again the doe leaped sideways. As she did, Bill caught sight of the translucent blue-gray sack. He looked for the front hoof, and there it was, followed by the left foot and leg with the little head pressed between the forelegs. The rest of the body followed quickly. Within a few minutes, the slippery package was lying in the straw. Bill gave a disappointed cry. There was no movement from the newborn creature. Through the translucent walls of the sack, Bill could see that it was no more than bones with the hide stretched over them. As he watched, the doe stepped between him and the kid, and he could see her head bob with the efforts of her industrious licking. Then a snuffling gasp and a weak bleat. How *could* that tiny body have life? Bill stepped closer and saw how very much alive it was. "You little skinny thing," he crooned as he slid his hand in wonder along the warm wet neck. As its mother licked the twitching creature, the hair began to stand out from its body, hiding the valleys between the bones.

"Looks like she's got a nice doe for you." The voice surprised

Bill, who hadn't heard Mr. Cothern come up behind him. He was leaning over the pen wall now, smiling. He always smiled.

"I can't have it," Bill blurted, grabbing his cane as he pushed past Mr. Cothern and out of the door. Some of the plastic had come untied from his cast; he stepped on it with his left foot and almost fell. He gripped the cane so that his knuckles turned white. He tried to reach the barn door before the tears came.

"Can't keep a kid from an unproven doe. Enough gambles in this business without taking a chance on feeding a first kid. Don't know how Matilda will milk, let alone what kind of milker her kid will be. Better say 'good-bye' to the little girl," Mr. Cothern shouted after Bill.

"Don't sell this kid. Please," he sobbed out as he slammed the barn door behind him. The door stood between Bill's sobs and Mr. Cothern's answer.

The sun was low. The damp March wind blew about him as Bill stumbled toward home leaning heavily on his cane. The top of the cast chafed his leg, and muscle ache spread through his whole body. He forced his legs to move. When he reached Mr. Rutherford's, he leaned his head against the corner post of the paddock fence and sobbed out his disappointment and exhaustion. As he rested, the pain lessened.

Friendly barking from the kennel by the house brought Bill's attention to Mr. Rutherford's setter. "It's okay, Blue. It's just me." Next a soft nicker made him turn his head, and he saw the Rutherford horses coming toward him out of the dusk. "You look hungry. Isn't your boss home yet?" As he asked, a plan occurred to him. He saw himself working for Mr. Rutherford, taking care of his horses, earning money, buying his kid in spite of his father. Determination was stronger than his pain. He had to start *now*, somehow take care of the horses tonight. Then he could ask Mr. Rutherford to advance him some money to buy his kid. *His* kid. Bill forced his legs to carry him to the barn.

He slowly filled the wheelbarrow. Luckily there wasn't much manure. Perhaps he could get it all out in one load. He pushed the heaped barrow across the ground in jerks, bracing himself on the handles while he stepped on his bad leg, then pushing from his good leg. With only one strong leg it was difficult to keep from lurching. He thought of his father's admonitions about "a lazy man's load." He wished he had not tried to do the whole job in one trip. It was too hard to hold the brimming wheelbarrow level. When he came to an uneven place in the ground, he stumbled. As the load shifted to the right, Bill fell between the shafts. The ground was wet and cold. He lay there, whimpering, too exhausted to cry out loud. It was nearly dark, only a yellow streak across the western horizon.

Blue had stopped barking long ago, but now he began again. This time the bark was deep and menacing. Bill raised his head. Had the falling wheelbarrow frightened the dog? That couldn't be it. Blue was looking down the road. In a moment Bill saw why. A nightmare figure was coming toward the kennel. In the fading light, Bill made out a small frame, clothes flapping like a scarecrow in the wind, furtive, moving in jerks. The Spook stood at the gate of Blue's kennel! The dog stopped barking.

Bill waited on the ground until, as far as he could see, the Spook was gone. Then, painfully, he pulled himself up and went to the kennel. He found Blue licking the floor, tongue circling his chops, tail wagging. He looked to Bill and scratched at the wire. There was a dark lump of something just outside the fence. When he leaned over, he saw that it was a small piece of hotdog that had apparently rolled through the mesh of the wire out of the dog's reach. Automatically Bill started to throw it through to Blue. He checked the impulse. Carefully he looked at the bit of meat in his hand. There was a hole in one end. Bill broke it open, and a small pellet fell to the ground. Then he realized: as he lay there watching, Blue had been poisoned. He reached for the kennel door, then found to his horror that it was padlocked. He stumbled to the barn, an adrenaline rush blocking his pain. He knew he needed to act quickly, yet he had no plan of action.

Blue's feed and dish were just inside the tack room on a table. Bill glanced over the familiar whistle, leash, and training collar. He fixed on something he had not noticed before, a small key on a nail above the feed dish. He took it. He clumped back to Blue's kennel. His cold fingers fumbled to fit the key to the lock. Finally it opened. In a moment Bill had Blue by the collar. He pulled the dog to the barn.

Bill knew Blue should vomit. Hopefully he looked around him as he stood just inside of the barn door. A hose was coiled neatly in the corner behind the door. Over and over he looked back to it as he waited for an idea. Then a plan flashed to him. He would need both hands to force the nozzle down Blue's throat. The horses' lead ropes were hanging on their accustomed nail. Bill took one and snapped it to the dog's collar, then tied the other end tightly against the ladder so that Blue could scarcely move his head. He turned the water on slowly, then forced Blue's muzzle open with one hand and the nozzle of the hose. It seemed that all the water was overflowing onto the floor. He tried to force the hose a little way down Blue's throat. After what seemed a long, long time, Bill felt him retch. Quickly he unsnapped the lead rope, and Blue vomited. Bill was surprised at the quantity of water the dog had swallowed. He noticed three pieces of the hotdog and was relieved to see that they were still whole. He took Blue by the collar and stumbled back to the kennel. As the gate clicked shut with the dog safe inside, Bill sank to the ground.

When he regained consciousness, the headlights of a car were glaring in his face. The door swung open, slammed shut, and a man stepped toward him. If he could have found the breath, Bill would have screamed. Then his mind became more alert, and he realized that Blue was barking a happy welcome.

Mr. Rutherford gently lifted Bill to his feet. "Here," the boy muttered sleepily, pushing the key and the bit of hotdog he had found outside Blue's pen into Mr. Rutherford's hand. "There's more in the barn. It's poisoned."

"Poison!" Mr. Rutherford exclaimed. Then, not waiting for an answer, "Bill, you're wet and cold as ice." He took off his coat and wrapped it around Bill.

"I'm real dirty."

"Coats can be cleaned," retorted Mr. Rutherford as he helped Bill to the car.

"You'd better get that poison. Something might eat it." His jaws were chattering so that he could hardly force the words between his teeth.

Mr. Rutherford started to ask questions, then looked at the shivering boy and went silently to the barn.

"I've put the meat in a can, Bill. Now tell me what happened while I drive you home."

Bill rested his head against the back of the seat and spoke slowly. "Matilda had her kid. I was walking back from Cothern's, and I thought maybe I could feed the horses..."

"With that cast on!"

"...but I fell down. I lay on the ground, and Mr. Crawley came to Blue's kennel. I made Blue vomit with the hose."

"Did you get it all, Bill?"

"I think so."

They were soon home, and Mr. Rutherford carried Bill up the back steps into the kitchen. His mother helped him upstairs to his bed, then brought him his dinner.

He stopped chewing a mouthful of pot roast when he heard the voices of Mr. Rutherford and his father rising through the register into his room.

"Your son has done me a very great service."

Bill envisioned Mr. Rutherford's impeccable exterior with

the mustache that sometimes made his smile hard to find, then remembered the warm comfort of his coat and the ride home in his warm car. Some of the kids called him stuck up, but Bill *knew*. So did his pa. "I'm glad Bill has been able to help you." The *Billy* was finally gone!

"I don't know yet how Bill found the key to the kennel, and it took great presence of mind to think of using the hose to overfill him with water. Blue's trial days are over, but now, since Julia died, his companionship means a great deal to me."

"My dog's no field trial champion like Blue, but she's a good one, and I know what you mean."

"You also have a son." Bill fixed on Mr. Rutherford's voice. "Crawley is dangerous. When I stopped in at the grain elevator last week to pick up some feed, I chanced to hear quite a story from a man from the rendering plant. He told me that Crawley had called him to remove a dead cow. He said that the cow, although poor like all Crawley's stock, was not old. The carcass was bruised and cut. He said it had been badly beaten. That, combined with starvation, had apparently killed it."

"He has a temper all right," agreed George. "A guy can't get more irrational than to kill his own stock. Do you know why Crawley had it in for your dog?"

"I hit a sow of his on the way home from work last January. I offered to pay him, but he wouldn't take less than a hundred dollars for it, much more than his thin old sow was worth, so I refused. He threatened my dog then, and I started locking the kennel when I left for town. I guess when he couldn't catch Blue on his land, he came to my place to wreak his havoc."

"Are you going to sue him? Of course Bill will be glad to be your witness."

"That I certainly will not do." Glenn Rutherford explained. "I strongly suspect that Crawley stayed nearby to see the results of his efforts. It's likely that he saw and recognized Bill."

"You mean you think he'd try to hurt Bill?"

Bill gulped a tasteless lump of meat he had forgotten to swallow.

"I only mean I do not trust him. George, in my profession I often hear of serious crimes committed by people who are considered by their neighbors as only 'a little strange.'"

After a pause, Bill's father said, "Crawley's not smart enough to make a good farmer. Now his abused land is making him as hard and used up as it is."

"He's a cruel man. Tell Bill not to mention any of this to his friends. Gossip gets around fast in this valley. If Crawley doesn't know Bill saw him, it's best to keep it that way." Bill heard the chair scrape. "Give this to Bill."

"Thank you. Thank you very much." Bill heard the back porch door close.

Slowly Bill finished his cold dinner.

Chapter 6

Deer Fly Comes Home

The sun was high before Bill opened his eyes the next morning. The first thing he saw was an envelope on the table beside his bed—with Mr. Rutherford's return address. Bill tore it open. A piece of pale blue paper fell to the sheet. *Thirty dollars!* The most money he had ever had!

As he stared at the check, Bill heard agile steps approach his door. He turned from the window expecting to see his father's usual poised-for-work tension. He saw, instead, a relaxed smile and a fresh spark in his blue eyes. "Just thought you might like a ride to the Cotherns' this morning. That is, unless you'd rather walk."

"You mean I can have the kid—Really?" Bill sat bolt upright and leaned against the headboard.

"I had a talk with Glenn Rutherford last night and again on the phone this morning. Your mother and I decided that you've done some growing up. We figured that if you're old enough to earn a kid, you're old enough to take care of one."

"Holy Catfish!" Bill fell back on his pillow, letting the news sink in.

His father sat on the edge of the bed. His eyes were steady; he pressed his mouth into a serious line. Was his father going to say something to spoil it? Bill wondered.

"Did Crawley see you at Mr. Rutherford's last night?" his father asked abruptly.

"I don't know. It was getting dark."

"We'll go on the assumption that he did. You see, Bill, that old man's gone strange living like a hermit the way he does on the thinnest farm in the county." His father paused, wrinkling up his forehead. "I want you to listen carefully. If Old Man Crawley thinks you know what he tried to do, you're in danger as much as Blue. Stay off his land absolutely. But if you see him on the road, greet him like everything is fine. Don't do anything to make him mad, and don't act like you're scared. Understand?"

"Yes. But what about Blue? Do you think Old Man Crawley'll try again?"

"No telling what he'll do, but from now on Blue is probably safe. Glenn is keeping him locked in the house."

"That's good news."

Bill listened silently while his father told him what he had already heard, then gave him firm instructions. "Don't ever tell anyone about what you did for Glenn Rutherford's dog last night. No telling what Mr. Crawley will do if he thinks you know his secrets. If you blab about it, the whole neighborhood will know. Everything clear?"

"Yes. How is Blue?"

"As good as ever. Glenn called this morning and told me to tell you there was enough strychnine in that meat to have killed him within an hour." Bill's father was smiling again as he clapped his son's shoulder. "Your mother and I know how you earned that kid. I hope our praise is enough so you won't need it from others," he said, then left the room.

The prospect of getting his kid was the only thing that got Bill out of bed. His leg muscles were so stiff and sore it was difficult for him to get into his pants. When he got to the table, pancakes were stacked up on his plate. "I'll call Jane and Sammy and we'll all go," his father said.

Jane would chatter all over his thoughts like some nervous squirrel, thoughts that would be spoiled if he tried to tell the whole family. Next, they had to wait while she got dressed. Finally they were in the car. The scenery that had passed like a slug the day before passed in an antelope dash.

"I helped when Matilda's kid was born. It's brown like a deer. Littlest brown thing you ever saw."

"Buck or doe?" his father questioned.

"I forgot to look, but Mr. Cothern saw right off it was a doe."

"I'd notice first thing," Jane put in. "Gee, aren't you excited? If I were getting a kid, I just wouldn't be able to stop talking ever."

"You can't anyway."

"I just can't wait to see it."

Why does she have to bubble all over everybody when she gets excited? Bill's thoughts were intense, often wordless. Now they would have to be more wordless than ever, even with Doug.

When the car stopped, Bill headed for the barn as fast as he could swing his new, but already dirty, cast.

He found Matilda still in the kidding pen. Her little doe peered timidly from between her forelegs. "I'm going to take your baby away from you," he said as he clumped into the pen, "but you couldn't keep her long anyway, so you shouldn't mind."

The nimble creature trotted into a corner as Bill approached. He picked her up and held her against his jacket. She gave a couple of half-hearted kicks, then turned her attention to nosing the strange face next to hers. The tiny muzzle tickled so much that Bill was laughing when his parents came into the pen with Mr. Cothern.

Sammy wiggled through the legs of the three adults and stood in front. "You lucky stiff!"

"I'll give you some of my caterpillars next summer," Jane consoled.

"Looks like Peg Leg's got my goat." Mr. Cothern had everyone laughing.

"Well, Bill, what do you say we get some milk for your baby and get on home?"

"You can take it from Matilda now. Your kid should get the colostrum anyhow. I'll get you a pail, and you can lead her to the milking stand."

"What's colostrum?" Sammy asked while Mr. Cothern went to get the pail.

"That's the first milk that comes after a kid is born. It's got things in it that help keep the kid from getting sick," his father explained.

"Pa, you can hold her," Bill said, passing the leggy armful to his father.

"Can I hold her now? Can I hold her?" Sammy jumped with eager impatience. Then his father let Sammy hold the kid while Bill led Matilda to the stand and squeezed out the yellowish fluid. He got about a quart.

"That won't last much more than a day. I'll give you a half gallon from this morning's milking."

"You don't have to give it to me. Just take it out of this." Bill handed him Mr. Rutherford's check. "I already signed it." Mr. Cothern gave a long low whistle.

"I'll have to go to the house to get change for this." He was back in a few minutes with milk from the cooler and Bill's change. "Ten dollars for the kid and forty cents for the milk. That leaves you nineteen sixty. Right?"

"Right." Bill pocketed the change and took the milk.

"In two or three weeks you can switch her over to cow's milk. See you around," Mr. Cothern shouted after them as they took the milk and got into the car.

Most of the way home Sammy fussed because he wanted a goat too. "Don't be silly," Bill admonished. "I couldn't have a kid when I was seven. Of course you're not old enough."

"I had a squirrel when I was nine, so you'll be old enough pretty soon," his sister said. "That is if you take care of it. Bill had rabbits when he was nine, but he just let them die."

"Cut it, will you? That doesn't go so good coming from someone who boiled her squirrel to death in a kettle of ketchup." When Jane began to cry, Bill regretted his hasty words. "I didn't really mean to say that. It just came out."

"That was so awful about the ketchup," Jane sobbed. "It's mean of you to remind me."

Mr. Brock slowed the car and pulled over to the side of the road. He stopped and looked back at the children. Bill ducked his head against the silky neck of the kid, dodging the daggers that shot from his father's eyes. No words were spoken. His father drove on.

It wasn't until they turned into the driveway that conversation was resumed. "Don't be in any hurry to feed her," Mr. Brock advised. "It's not easy to bottle-feed a kid when she's used to nursing the doe, so let her get good and hungry."

When he got home, Bill escaped from Jane and Sammy and took his kid to the barn. Until lunchtime he hid with it in the feed alley behind the calf pens. There, where no one could see him, he could rub his cheek against the soft hair and breathe the sweet newborn smell. "You need a name," he murmured, moving his hand thoughtfully over her fawn-colored hair. "I could call you Fawnie." Somehow the name didn't please him. As he lay in the clean straw, he was startled by a buzzing. Had it been later in the spring, he wouldn't have given a thought to the sound, but now it held the promise of summer. His eye followed the buzz, and he saw a large iridescent fly strike the dusty glass of a small window above his head. Something about the flighty speed and zigzag movements of the fly reminded Bill of the angular prancing of a kid. "Deer Fly," he announced suddenly. "Your name is Deer Fly. Sort of like a deer and sort of like a fly."

Bill wanted to tell the family, and besides it must be lunchtime. He was hungry.

Before he came into the kitchen, his mother made him put the kid under an overturned basket in the back room with newspapers underneath. They ate to the background music of Deer Fly's forlorn bleating. During the meal Bill didn't let the conversation drift away from the subject of kids. They covered every aspect of kid feeding and decided to begin the project after lunch.

Bill put about three quarters of a cup of Matilda's colostrum in a nursing bottle, heated it in a pan of hot water, then rushed to his bleating kid. Much to his consternation she fought the proffered refreshment like a grown mule. After fifteen minutes of struggling, Bill returned the bottle, still half full, to the refrigerator. Most of the missing half had spilled out of the kid's mouth where it remained to sour on her muzzle and chest. Later in the afternoon Bill reheated the bottle and tried again. This time nothing would come out of the nipple.

"Colostrum thickens when it stands around," his father explained to Bill when he went to him for advice. "You'd better heat some water and dilute the milk a bit."

Bill followed the advice. This time he got another tablespoon or so down Deer Fly's reluctant throat, and much more outside.

By late afternoon, the kid was bleating continuously for the food she refused to take. Bill was beginning to wonder if his prize was worth the effort when his father walked into the house after milking to wash and read the paper before supper. He took in the situation at a glance. "If it doesn't cause you a little sweat, it's not worth having."

"Then she's sure worth having."

"Come now, if you're smart as a goat, you'll find a way to get milk down her gullet. You got the liquid down Blue all right."

"She's pretty dumb if she won't eat," Bill grumbled. His father was reading the paper now. Bill dejectedly rubbed Deer Fly's ears. He sighed and put the bottle back in the refrigerator. "Think I'll show Deer Fly to Mr. Rutherford," he said.

"Don't you think you've had enough walking for the day?" his mother asked.

"Aw, I'm not tired. I rested just about all day."

"You have a pretty funny idea of resting, but you can go if you hurry back. We're going to eat in half an hour."

Bill put on his jacket and buttoned it over the kid. He had no sooner reached the highway when a car pulled to a stop along side of him. "May I give you a ride?" Mr. Rutherford called.

"Thanks," Bill answered as he eagerly got into the car. "I was coming to show you. Look what I got. I paid for it with the check you gave me. Thanks a heap. Her name's Deer Fly."

"Well, well, well, so Matilda gave you a doe. A mighty pretty one she is too, what I can see of her."

Bill unbuttoned his jacket and let the kid stand on his lap. "I helped Matilda have her yesterday." Deer Fly quavered the air with a bleat.

"She sounds hungry. What do you feed her?" Mr. Rutherford asked as he got out of the car to open the garage door. After the car was put away Bill told him of the struggles of the afternoon.

"Why don't you try letting her suck a cow," he suggested. "Even though it's not as good for her as goat's milk, it's better than nothing."

"Thanks. Thanks a lot. I'll try it right now." Mr. Rutherford smiled after the retreating boy.

As he passed the Crawley place, the Spook hailed him. "What'cha got in your jacket, boy?"

Bill remembered his father's warning. He swallowed hard, then answered. "A kid. How are you, Mr. Crawley?"

"A kid? What for?"

"A pet."

By now the Spook was nearly up to him, and Bill could smell his rotten breath as he exclaimed, "A pet! A kid's real good eatin' if they's milk fed, but they ain't good for nothin' else but butcherin'. Maybe you'll let me taste yours sometime, eh?"

"I've got to hurry home. I'm late for supper." Bill clutched the bleating kid close and hobbled as fast as he was able. To his relief, the Spook didn't follow.

Although the kitchen door had closed behind Bill, he didn't feel that Crawley had been shut out. It would be hard to tell his parents how it was. "Something spooky happen..." he began, but they were all bent over some map Jane was drawing for extra credit, so they weren't listening to him.

"I'm going to put in all our neighbors, our whole community," she explained.

"That's an ambitious project. You have a good start though."

"I know. It's going to take a long time."

"I like the careful way you've drawn the fences."

Finally his mother finished raving about the map and turned to Bill. "How did Mr. Rutherford like Deer Fly?"

"He liked her fine, and he knows how to feed her too. He said we should put her on a cow."

"Might work," Mr. Brock said, getting up from his chair.

"Don't go out now," Bill's mother pleaded as she saw her husband putting on his jacket.

"A good farmer always feeds his livestock before he feeds himself." George smiled and kissed his wife as he passed her.

When they reached the bottom of the steps, the small stringy-haired border collie came to heel behind her master. Bill didn't care for the dog. She worked only for his father. With everyone else—except Sammy—she was shy and cringing. "Pa, how come Annie isn't scared of stock when she's scared stiff of people?" Bill asked.

"I don't know that anyone has the exact answer to that one, but the way I figure it there's a chunk of wild animal in some strains of dogs. Like wolves they figure that man is their natural enemy, and livestock is their natural prey. The killing has been bred out of them, but the stalking is left in. A border collie eyes the cattle the way he does and stalks like a crouching cat because his insides tell him to, not because he loves the stock. It takes a lot of patience to win the confidence of a shy one like Annie, but once you've got it, she figures you're sort of another dog, a smart one that she'll obey the same way her ancestors obeyed their pack leader. Dogs don't think they're people like some folks tell you. They think their boss is top dog."

"Then why does she like Sammy?" asked Bill. "He's too little to lead anything."

"She's got Sammy figured as a puppy in the pack, and all pack members protect the puppies."

They reached the barn. Mr. Brock snapped the light switch as two long lines of white and tawny faces turned in their stanchions and gazed placidly at Bill and his father. "Let's take the little Guernsey in the far corner. She's got the smallest teats, so Deer Fly should be able to get her mouth around them okay."

Bill took the stool his father handed him and squatted close to the belly of the cow. He nudged the udder a few times, then ran his fingers down the teats to start the flow of milk. A small black cat stalked over to Bill, meowing for a piece of the action.

"Okay, Blossom. You'll get your reward for all those mice you catch." Bill squirted a stream of milk into the cat's open mouth. "Now it's Deer Fly's turn." With his free hand, he raised the kid's muzzle to the cow. Tentatively she put out an exploring tongue. Then she sucked!

At his father's insistence, Bill left Deer Fly in the calf pen, then returned to the house with a light heart and a hungry stomach.

Chapter 7

Meet Brighty

Bill came into the kitchen, an empty nursing bottle in his hand. Feeding problems were over.

Mrs. Brock stood at the kitchen sink washing asparagus; Jane was breaking off the white ends as the April sun splashed over their hands. "Doug called while you were outside. I told him you'd call back."

This was going to be a good Saturday. Bill went to the phone in high spirits. The doctor had sawed off his cast last week. Now, with two good legs, he could keep pace with the spring surge of life.

On his bike Doug arrived at Bill's in minutes. "What do we do today?" he demanded, his black eyes darting like a warbler's flight. "Work on the tree house?"

Heads together in earnest conversation, the two boys went off to collect hammers, nails, and lumber. On the way to the machine shed, they untied Deer Fly. She trotted contentedly after them, pausing to nibble tasty buds from shrubs and plants. She had known her own kind for only fifteen short hours, so had easily adopted the boys as her rightful herd. When left alone, she bleated almost continuously.

Winter's vigor and summer's languor mingled in the air. The

boys, after an energetic burst of carpentering, lay on their backs on the nearly finished platform gazing at the firecracker-red tridents swinging over their heads. "Never noticed maples had flowers as pretty as this," said Bill.

Doug reached to pick one. "Neither did I." It was too cold to remain still long. "Let's play tag with Deer Fly," Doug suggested. After the boys swung down the rope ladder Doug ran for the pile of concrete blocks behind the barn. The light-footed Deer Fly gamboled after him while Bill limped a little behind. At four weeks his kid was half grown, poised on slender spring-rods. She could sunfish with an agility that made a bronc look like an elephant by comparison. The three climbed to the top of the block pile, then Bill lowered his round head to meet Deer Fly's pointed one. They laughed and chased, all three kids, one goat, two human.

"Hey, Bill, come help me load the spreader." Mr. Brock's words put an end to the morning's fun and caused Bill to drag his feet toward the idling tractor. Doug headed for home.

His father set Bill to raking the litter out of the chicken house, a job he hated. The stink of ammonia was so strong it made his eyes water. The work had scarcely begun before Doug returned shouting, "Hey, Bill. Deer Fly's following me. Want me to tie her up?"

"Yeah. Her stake's in front of the house. Just snap the chain to her collar."

"Now that spring's coming, you're going to have to be careful with that goat, Bill. You know how much damage she could do in a garden."

"Sure, I know." But Bill wasn't thinking so much about the damage the kid might do as he was about the damage the Spook could do to the kid. As he recalled the Spook's talk of butchering, he relaxed his hold on the fork.

"Bill!"

61

At the snap of his name, Bill again bent over his task with a labored sigh and a faraway look in his eyes.

"You'll never make a farmer, or anything else either, if you don't learn to keep your mind on your work."

"I don't much want to keep my mind on chicken shit."

"If you don't like it this way, think of what happens when it's spread on the garden. How about corn on the cob?"

"I don't mind thinking of this stuff changing into corn, just so I don't think of the stink of this shit in August when I'm eating the corn."

"You know," his father continued after a short pause, "everything alive comes out of the dirt. All that goat of yours is is dirt and manure mixed up with a dash of God's air and water chemistry. Just chew on that for awhile."

When Bill managed a smile the lines around George Brock's mouth transformed into contented furrows.

* * *

"Hey, Bill," Doug suggested a few weeks later, "think we could get Deer Fly up into the tree house?"

"Say, that's an idea," Bill responded. Together the two boys pulled and pushed the unwilling goat up the rope ladder. Once on the platform, she seemed as much at home as the boys and immediately began nibbling the young maple leaves.

"Deer Fly likes it here, doesn't she?"

"Of course," Bill answered. "Goats are mountain animals, so she likes high places. She likes the tops of cars too," he added ruefully.

"Her hoofs are still pretty soft though, so they shouldn't scratch too much."

"Pa doesn't even like little scratches."

"At least he'll let you have a pet. My pa won't let me keep anything. Not even a dog... Say, those jays have just about finished their nest," Doug observed, looking down at the casual pile of twigs in the cedar below the tree house.

"They sure are sloppy about it," Bill commented.

"Hey, look at Deer Fly's cud." Doug was watching the gravity-defying lump rise like a ball on a string up the slender throat. "Would be handy to gulp down your food and then bring it up to chew when you didn't have anything better to do, wouldn't it?" The boys watched the grinding jaws and listened to the muffled belch while Deer Fly peacefully brought up her cud to the boys' guttural imitations of airplane motors. Then, tiring of the restricted location, she walked to the edge of the platform. After carefully calculating the height, she jumped.

"Golly!" the boys exclaimed in unison as the goat landed softly as a cat, then trotted over to the house. Annie was barking at the approaching bottle-gas truck as Deer Fly joined her. Teasingly the kid presented her stubby horns, then rose over the dog as if to strike with her forelegs. Annie stood her ground, crouching, then glaring at the kid. Deer Fly, with a casual toss of her head, trotted after the bottle-gas man, nibbling at his clothes as he worked. Amused, he rubbed her neck and tickled her muzzle before getting back into his truck. Deer Fly rose lightly to the hood, then bounded down the other side as the driver slid onto the seat and slammed the door. The boys nearly rolled off the platform in their laughter, but Bill's subsided quickly when he saw her chase the truck down the road. "Jeepers, the next stop is Mr. Rutherford's. Think she'll follow all the way?" Bill wondered.

"You bet she will. Look at her gallop will you!" exclaimed Doug.

The boys couldn't see the Rutherford farm from the tree house, but in a few minutes they did see the truck turn back up the Brock's drive. They climbed down from the tree and ran to meet the driver.

"Thought you might want your kid back," he said, opening the door and shoving the goat at the boys.

"Gee, thanks," Bill said. "Sorry she was so much bother."

"That's okay. Breaks the monotony. First time I've ever had a goat chase me. At least she doesn't bite at the wheels." He drove off laughing while the boys led the kid to her tether.

* * *

Bill watched the bottoms of Doug's bare feet as he crawled from the rope ladder to the platform. Leaves screened the boys from the farmyard. The chickens were scratching for bugs and seeds, Deer Fly was nibbling grass, Sammy was loading twigs into his toy dump truck, his pa was planting corn.

"You can see lots of stuff from a tree house," Doug said.

"Yeah. We're on top of everybody else."

"I mean right close." Doug was looking intently at the jay's nest in the cedar below them.

"I see a jay egg if that's what you mean," Bill answered indifferently.

"Yeah, but it wasn't there last time we looked."

"So what. Sooner or later there're going to be jay eggs in a jay's nest. Jays are no good anyway. They just eat other birds' eggs and even babies."

"Aw, don't be such a wet blanket. Even a jay's good for something if he happens to be in the right place at the right time. They can be real brave. I saw one chase a squirrel away from his nest one time."

"I don't like the noisy things," Bill said. "You can have 'em."

For the next three days all Doug did was lie on his stomach on the platform looking down into the nest. On the third day he shouted to Bill who was watering Deer Fly, "Now there are three!"

On a Friday afternoon two weeks later, as Doug was riding

his bike into the Brocks' yard, the jays screamed an alarm. "Hey, Bill, something's up!" he exclaimed as the calls continued. Bill followed the sound to the cedar beside the tree house and watched Doug climb to the nest. The birds were now dividing their attention between their nest and Doug's head. He waved them off with his hands and continued his climb. A feathery branch over his head hid his view of the nest. He grasped it, pulled his chin over it and looked up. "A snake!" he shouted. Bill caught a glimpse of the black and yellow coils of a bull snake wrapped around the nest. The yellow throat rose up, and a forked tongue flicked to taste the air. Doug straddled the branch, then broke off a twig. He waved it teasingly in front of the snake's hissing mouth. When it struck, he grabbed the snake just behind the head and pulled it from the nest. "One egg is okay," Doug shouted. He threw the snake to the ground and took the egg. Holding it carefully in his hand, he climbed a couple of branches down, then handed the egg to Bill. They watched the snake slide into the tall grass. "Wish I'd killed that sneaky snake," Doug said.

"Pa wouldn't have liked it if you had. He says bull snakes get a lot more mice and gophers than they do birds."

"Not this one," Doug countered.

"Look!" exclaimed Bill, who had been examining the speckled egg, "It's cracked."

"Aw shucks. I thought I'd saved one anyhow."

"I don't mean it's busted. It's pecking out."

"Give it back. It's mine."

"Don't get so impatient. I'm going to."

Bill handed the egg back to Doug, who held it in his cupped hands and waited. The boys sat on the ground leaning against the trunk of the cedar; their hair mingled as they bent over the egg. Little by little, the tiny beak chopped its way around the shell, and the top half fell off like a cap, revealing the scrawny naked chick.

"Gol, but he's dinky!" Doug exclaimed with a small birdlike laugh.

Its skin had a sickly bluish cast. "Don't see how that awful-looking little scarecrow could grow up to be as pretty as his pa," Bill said. "What'cha going to do with him?"

"I don't know. We can't put him back. Maybe his parents wouldn't take care of him, and besides that snake might be back."

Both boys listened to the tiny peeps in silence.

"I know. I'll raise him," Doug announced.

"Yeah," Bill agreed. "You could feed him chick starter. That oughta work. Jays eat seeds and bugs, same as chickens."

"Have you got some?" Doug got to his feet.

The boys ran to the chicken house and filled their pockets with starter mash. Doug took a pinch of it and sprinkled a little into the gaping beak. "Golly, he's all mouth, isn't he?" The dust of the grain stuck to the lining of its throat, and none went down the gullet.

"I know," suggested Bill. "Spit on it first. That's what the mother jay does."

Doug spit into his palm and stirred in the grain with his little finger. "Here goes, zoooom." He dive-bombed the beak, and the creature swallowed vigorously. "Hey, he wants my finger too."

"Let me do it." Bill reached for Doug's palm.

Reluctantly Doug let him have a turn, then gave more of the mash himself. "Gee, I wish Deer Fly had eaten like that!"

"What'cha got?" Sammy had come up unnoticed. Excitedly Doug told the story. "Can I feed him now?" Sammy asked.

His brother answered. "No, he's had enough, and anyhow you're too little."

"I am not, you, you dirty double disconnected semicircle

66

sewer pipe." Sammy dissolved in tears. "You'll be sorry," he sputtered as he ran toward the house.

"Tattle tale, tattle tale, tattle tale tit," Bill sang after him.

"I'm not going to tattle. I'm going to do something. Something you won't like."

"Now," Doug said, getting back to the business at hand, "I've got to have a place to keep him warm."

"How about a sort of nest under your shirt?"

"Good idea." The boys got to work making a pouch out of a piece of the skirt from an old saddle. The leather was thin, almost worn through where the stirrup leather rubbed against it, so it wasn't too stiff to work. Bill got a leather punch from the machine shed. They took turns punching holes in the leather and holding and feeding the bird. After the pouch was finally ready they strung it together with an old bootlace, and Doug filled it with chicken down and strapped it under his shirt with his belt. The sun was low in the sky when Doug rode off with his new responsibility under his shirt and his pockets full of chick starter.

Chapter 8

Revenge

When Doug left, Bill headed toward the house with the intention of moving Deer Fly's stake to fresh grass. Although she hadn't had time to crop all the grass in the old location, she was too fastidious to eat what she had trampled. Funny, thought Bill. I'm sure I left her by the elm. Then he saw the stake and chain. How could she have gotten away? He continued toward the house.

On the porch stood Sammy, pulling nervously at Annie's ears. "I told you I was going to do something," he said, surprised and frightened by the terrible expression on Bill's face. He was even showing his teeth like a mad dog.

"Jane, Jane," called Sammy as he saw his brother coming toward him, arm raised, teeth clenched. Halfway to the goal, Bill changed his mind.

"Don't run, Sammy. Tell me something. Has a car been here?"

"Just Mr. Cothern to get that milk can you didn't take back to him." Bill raced down the road shouting his kid's name as he ran. Opposite the Spook's vegetable garden, Bill came to a terror-stricken halt. The unconcerned Deer Fly was grazing contentedly down a row of corn. Bill saw at a glance that she had taken almost all of the new shoots. He also saw that the Spook was approaching her, a hay fork above his head.

Bill drew in his breath and called, "Come, Deer Fly. Come, girl." The kid's head snapped up at the familiar call. The corn was good, but Bill would have something better in his pocket. He never yet had failed her. She trotted to him as he turned and ran, but not faster than the Spook's threat.

"If I ever see that stinking goat around my place again, I'll butcher it, I will. It's my rights."

Sammy wasn't in sight when Bill ran into the yard, Deer Fly beside him. His father was standing on the porch. "I'm glad to see you got your kid."

The wide-eyed fear in Bill's expression told his father where Deer Fly had been. "She got almost all Crawley's sweet corn," Bill blurted out. "Where's Sammy?"

"Sammy is not your concern," his father answered sternly. "You know as well as I do that he didn't know what he was doing."

"But what are you going to do about him? He just can't do it again. The Spook'll kill Deer Fly. You should have heard him!"

"Your mother and I will do our best with Sammy. Now I'll have to tell Mr. Crawley that we'll give him all the corn he can use when ours comes in."

"Can I go with you?" Bill wondered why he wanted to go, scared as he was.

"No. It's absolute. I don't want you on the Crawley place even with me. I'll go alone tonight after we eat. Your ma's waiting supper, so come on in as soon as you tie up the kid."

His father's tread on the steps, the clinking of Deer Fly's chain, the bleat of anticipation when he brought her a measure of grain—they were familiar sounds of home. But Bill's fear took all the comfort out of them, leaving nothing as it should be.

Rays of the low sun swept the undersides of a line of cirrus clouds. He leaned against the porch door and thought about the sun, that bloodred splash across the sky. Just about all the energy there is comes from that far-off ball of fire: green plants die without it, animals die without the green plants. He would die too. Now the sun was splashing blood, like the day dying. At noon it packed a punch that would make him blind if he dared to look too long. The earth could store that punch like a root cellar stores garden stuff for winter. His pa had told him so the afternoon he had helped clean up the fencerow and burn the brush. The next evening the heat that belonged to the sun was still glowing under the ashes. The family was toasting marshmallows over the coals when his father said, "The sun's working overtime tonight. That fire's releasing the sun's energy stored fifty years ago. It's still the sun that's warming us."

Bill's mind skipped to stuff in Sunday school about "dust to dust" and "life everlasting." Now the Spook made the dust part too real. He ran the fingers of his hand along his arm and looked down at his skin, just a thin cover for all those bones and muscles and blood and guts. Just a house of blocks the sun built for fun. Easy to knock it down, just what the Spook would like. The secret danger Bill held inside made the sun's blood in the sky his own. The sun wouldn't care. It could build new life out of the blocks death knocked down. *Everlasting* was too far away to give him comfort.

"Pst."

Like a cornered fox, Bill crouched and spun. Slowly, he relaxed. "That you, Doug?"

"Yeah."

"Jeepers, you don't have to scare a guy to death." Bill laughed, but it only covered the surface of his thoughts. "What do you want?"

"Have you had supper yet? Nobody's home at my house, so I thought maybe I could eat here. Huh?"

"I guess so." Bill went into the house while Doug loitered on the steps. "Ma, can Doug stay for supper?"

His mother set a dish of bread-and-butter pickles on the table. "Yes, there's plenty. Jane called and said she won't be home for supper, so Doug can sit in her place." Then she muttered in an undertone, "That poor boy, he might as well not have a mother, working the way she does at Joe's Steak House every night."

Bill poked his head out the door. "It's okay," he called to Doug who, with a glowing face, bounded into the kitchen perfumed with baking pecan rolls. He certainly didn't look like the "poor boy" Mrs. Brock had been pitying.

"Meet Bright Eyes. Brighty for short," he announced, unbuttoning his shirt and holding open the mouth of his leather pouch. Bill's mother looked down into the pink cavern of the tiny gullet.

"Oh, isn't it cute. But so young! Do you think you can raise it?"

"Sure. Brighty eats good. Watch this." Doug took a pinch of chick starter from his pocket, put it in his palm and spat on it. He scooped up a bit on his little finger, then thrust it down the ever-hungry gullet. He hunched his shoulders in an ecstasy of suppressed laughter as the tickley feeling traveled up his finger to his arm.

"Sticky rolls!" Sammy exclaimed as Mrs. Brock took the sheet of rolls from the oven and filled the serving plate while Mr. Brock admired the bird. "Come to the table, boys. Your ma's been waiting supper."

Mr. Brock was the last to sit. He let himself down slowly as if sitting were an unnatural position. Something about it must have hit Doug's funny bone, and his laughter exploded. He clutched both hands to his mouth in an effort to hold it in. A few snickers escaped during grace, then mouthfuls of chicken pie and rolls stopped up conversation until Doug's voice came through, fuzzy like the clapper of a bell wrapped in cotton. "Think chick starter's the best thing to feed him, Mrs. Brock?"

"Yes, I should think that would be all right. But it might be a good idea to give the little fellow a variety. Then if something he needs is missing from the chick starter, he'll get it from the other things you give him."

"Jays'll rob other birds' nests sometimes, so how about giving him egg? You could use an eyedropper. That should work swell," said Bill.

His mother suggested, "It would be easier, I think, to hard-boil the egg and give Brighty the yolk moistened with a little water."

"Hey, I've got a real good idea!" exclaimed Sammy. "You could give him real soft pieces of worm. Birds always like 'em."

"Aw, be quiet," said Bill. "You're too little to know anything about anything." Even while he was speaking, Bill was confused and sorry. He knew it wasn't Sammy that kept him on edge.

"I am not. I know a little about a little."

"Bill!"

"I'm sorry, Sammy." He turned toward his father's stern face.

"Sammy has as much right to speak his mind as you or I, and he has as much right to be listened to politely as you or I. What's more, it just so happens that this time he has a pretty good idea. Tomorrow you and Doug can go out to the garden and pick cabbage worms. If you can't find any, you can catch those white butterflies. I noticed a few yesterday, and they should be just as good as worms."

Doug looked doubtful. "Don't you think wings would be kind of indigestible?" he asked.

"Oh boy! Strawberry shortcake!" Sammy bounced up and down in his chair.

The rest of the chicken and asparagus slid quickly down the assembled throats while anticipating eyes watched Mrs. Brock whipping the cream.

Doug's question seemed to have been forgotten. "What about the wings?" he repeated.

"You'd probably better take them off. They'd be kind of hard to get down," Mr. Brock advised. "But this shortcake sure goes down nice," he added.

"I'm glad you prefer it to butterfly wings," his wife responded with a smile. "I don't have any recipes for those."

When they finished eating Mr. Brock scraped back his chair and stood up. "I'll be going out for awhile," he said abruptly as he walked across the kitchen. The screen door banged behind him. What would Pa say to Crawley? What will that crawling Spook do? How will he take the offer of corn from our garden? As these questions circled in Bill's mind, his curiosity crowded out fear of the Spook that had so possessed him early in the evening. His desire to know was overwhelming. He just had to have action or all the stuff inside him would explode like too much air in a balloon.

"Well, how about it?" Doug shouted, his voice finally penetrating Bill's consciousness.

"How about what?"

"What I just said," came the impatient answer.

Mrs. Brock looked at the boys standing between the table and the sink. "Would you two clear the table please? I couldn't possibly break through your line without someone to run interference for me."

"We'll get out of the way," Bill said quickly.

"Oh no you won't. You'll clear the table."

As they shuffled from sink to table, Doug repeated his proposition to Bill.

"Like I said before, you dimwit. Walk home with me, and

we'll fish the stream. There's going to be a full moon, so it'll be real light."

Another plan had been forming in Bill's mind, and Doug didn't fit in. "Can't tonight. I've got to take care of Deer Fly."

"That won't take long. Anyhow you can bring her with."

"Yeah, but I've got some chores to do after that."

"Okay then. I'll see you tomorrow." Doug banged out the door. "Bye, Mrs. Brock. Thanks for the good supper." The words floated back into the house through the open window.

Bill heard his mother's "Good-bye, Doug. Come again!" as he followed Doug out the door and watched Doug's bike bounce off down the gravel road, the back fender shaking out its last supporting screw. "Brighty must feel like he's in an earthquake," Bill shouted after his retreating pal.

Chapter 9

Rabbits Don't Imagine

Bill walked slowly down the driveway as he planned those mysterious "chores" he had told Doug he must do. "The first part is easy," he muttered, walking faster. "The oak woods will give me plenty of cover." Bill ran along the edge of the oat field, then crossed the road to the Mason side. If he were to reach the Crawley place in time to find out what the Spook planned to do to Deer Fly, he would have to hurry. He soon reached the fence between the Masons' field and the Crawley woods and rolled under the wire. As he made his way through the tangle of blackcap canes that edged the woods, he remembered his father's warning: "You're in danger, son. Stay off his land absolutely." There was no misconstruing those words. *But I gotta hear with my own ears*, he thought as he stepped into the moonlit woods. He was on the Spook's land.

Bill wove his way swiftly through the oaks and birches. The leaf mold was damp and soft under his feet. Except for the snap of an occasional stick and the brush of a leafy branch, his progress was silent. The woods thinned and were replaced by chokecherry, wild plum, and sumac. The next lap of the way would be along the fence line between the Spook's pasture and the black expanse of a field newly prepared for planting. The burdock and other weeds and brush that grew along the unkempt fencerow offered good protection, but rough going. By the time he reached the corner, Bill's clothes were matted with the weathered gray porcupines of last year's burdock. A small bur oak grew at the corner of the pasture directly behind the Spook's house. Bill crouched behind it. He could hear the hum of voices coming from the front of the house. As he listened, he nervously fingered a fringed acorn cup. He was too far away. He couldn't hear. He straightened up behind the tree, put the acorn cup in his pocket, and peered toward the house. The men must be in front. He couldn't see them. Ahead of him and a little to his right was the body of an old Ford truck. It was against the south side of the house. In the shadow, Bill couldn't get a good look at it, but he had often seen it from the road, so could fill in the details the shadow blotted out. He remembered that the wheels were missing so that he couldn't get under it. Also the left door was missing, allowing him to climb in without making any noise. Yes, it would be a good place to hide if he could just get across the open stretch of moon-white ground between it and his vantage point behind the tree.

He hesitated, knowing that if the two men happened to walk around the corner of the house he would be seen—and recognized. He clung to the tree and strained to hear the words his father and the Spook were speaking. Their voices were low; he could understand only an occasional word. "...so possibly..." That was his father. "...I don't..." That was the Spook. It was tantalizing. He ducked low and ran. As he dove through the gaping side and under the cracked steering wheel, he heard the voices coming toward him around the corner of the house. "You know I'm sorry about the damage that's been done," his father said.

Did the Spook see me running? Cautiously Bill raised his head above the dashboard and looked out between the forks of jagged glass, all that remained of the windshield. His left hand gripped the steering wheel, his right was braced against the pile of feed bags tossed in a haphazard pile on the bare springs of the seat.

"Don't want no corn of yours." His rasping voice grated in Bill's ears. "What I want is your boy to help me with the chores at night."

"I'm sorry. I couldn't do that. I need him myself in the evening."

Bill was reassured by his father's polite refusal, but the Spook persisted in a tone that was barely civil on the surface. As he listened, a shiver vibrated down Bill's spine the way it did when one of the boys at school scraped his knife on the blackboard. "Then let him come at noon."

"No, school isn't out yet, so he can't do that."

"Then after school is out."

Fear blanked out his father's answer as he watched, almost hypnotized, while the crooked fingers of a gnarled hand reached and grasped the radiator cap. How could he have failed to notice how close the Spook had come? Should the old man turn his eyes, Bill would be sure to be seen. His head was in the full glow of the moon. He crouched, and as he crouched, his left hand slid over the steering wheel. A terrifying blast hit his ears. He collapsed in a trembling heap on the floor, pulling a pile of feed sacks over him as he went down. The seconds of silence that followed were worse than the blast of the horn. He heard steps approaching the side of the truck next to the house. The rusty door squeaked open on one hinge, and Crawley's thick breathing was directly over him. The thud of something flung with violent force vibrated through the springs beside him. Then a loud pained cry. Bill gripped his legs to him in a ball of terror. He had apparently cried out without knowing that he did so, like pieces of himself fighting against him. Then he heard the Spook.

"There she goes. It's that cussed cat. She must have jumped on the horn getting in here to her kittens. Scared me near to death." Slowly Bill realized the cat, not he, had screamed. Bill huddled on the floor waiting for his strength to return.

Clouds covered the moon. It was inky dark when he moved silently toward home.

* * *

The kitchen door slammed behind Bill. As he walked, blinking, across the polished floor, he felt as though he were on a stage. The spotlights shone down at him from the ceiling, and the reflecting floor supplied the footlights. His mother put down the sock she was darning. His father put down *The Farm Journal*.

"Where have you been?"

Bill had prepared no answer. "Oh, just out," he stammered. "Out for a walk." He ducked through the door and tramped up the stairs to his room. He got ready for bed, leaving his bur matted clothes in a heap on the bathroom floor, then slipped between the sheets carefully, as always, so that the bed would be as easy as possible to make in the morning.

The moon hung behind the cottonwood outside Bill's window. The shivering leaves made an agitated pattern against it. Bill turned his head from the window, but the sound was as restless as the sight. Thoughts rustled in his mind, half-formed like the moonlit leaves. He was as awake as the out-of-doors. He turned to his stomach, and the bed pad bunched under him. His parents were coming up the stairs. A ribbon of light sifted under the door; the voices increased the night's disturbance.

He heard the bathroom door open. "Where do you think he got all those burs?" his mother asked.

"Not on my farm," came his father's decisive answer.

Why did I leave my clothes on the bathroom floor? Bill lamented.

"Pockets full, as usual. His knife, a goldfinch's wing, milk tickets, and I don't know what all."

Bill heard the wastebasket clatter against the bathtub.

"Here's an acorn cup," his mother went on, "and chick starter over everything."

"He looked guilty as a chicken-killing dog when he walked through that kitchen," his father said. "That acorn cup's from a bur oak, isn't it? Looks like a fringe on it from here."

"Yes, I guess so, but what difference does that make? Where do you think he went?"

"I don't know, but I've got a pretty good idea. If I'm right, I'll know for sure in the morning. We don't have bur oaks; I know who does."

His mother was speaking, but the running water hid the words.

A whip-poor-will was calling. Bill heard his parents' door open and close. The call of the whip-poor-will came closer. Bill slept a little, then saw the Spook's hand swinging a milk stool at him. He turned to run, and his father was standing on red earth against a red sky with a cottonwood branch in his hand. "Whip-poor-Bill, whip-poor-Bill," the bird was singing, and Bill woke up. It was a long time before he went to sleep for good.

★ ★ ★

Bill's mother called him. When she called again he got out of bed slowly, dressed and went down to breakfast. "No, I don't want eggs." He munched halfheartedly on a piece of toast.

He wiped the jelly from his mouth. "Your father wants to see you. He's cultivating," his mother said curtly. Bill put down his napkin. It fell to the floor. He went outside.

The engine from the faraway tractor sounded gentle on the air. He could go a little later. Bill headed toward Deer Fly's stake. He gave her water, but she did little more than dip her muzzle.

He moved her to fresh grass, but she wasn't in the mood for grazing. She hopped to the end of her tether, then came back to Bill in a series of popcorn bounces. She stopped quietly in front of him and nibbled the tip off a stalk of pigweed. "I'll get you something better than that." Bill went to the granary and returned shortly with a pan of oats and cracked corn and soy beans. He sat on a patch of clover and talked to her as she ate.

"Deer Fly..." She raised her head, and he scratched her under the jaw. "You're my best friend and the only one I can talk to." The kid buried her nose in the feed pan and munched contentedly. "You don't know how lucky you are, Baby. If you had as many worries as I do, you wouldn't care whether you ate or not. The Spook's trying to get me, and he'd like to kill us both. Oh, why'd you have to eat his corn?" Bill put his arms around the kid's neck and pushed his face against her sleek hair, breath catching in his throat as he pressed his forehead hard against Deer Fly.

"Hi there, old boy," came a jaunty shout behind him.

He hadn't heard Doug approaching, and he waited a few seconds to be sure his voice would come out right before turning his head to say "Hi."

Doug's words tumbled in an eager avalanche. "The folks didn't get in 'till after I got to bed, and I was out before they got up, so they still don't know I've got Brighty. I don't s'pose they'd let me keep him if they knew."

"Go fishing last night?" Bill asked disinterestedly.

"Yeah. Got a nice one too. Kim was down there. He's got a new fly rod, but the only thing he could catch was leaves off the trees. Threw his line all over the place." As he talked, Doug was reaching his hand into his pocket. His jeans were tight, and it took a little squirming to get his hand in. "See. Isn't she a nice one?" he asked triumphantly, pulling from his pocket a four-inch trout, dry and stiff.

"Yeah. It's okay."

"Thought Brighty might like a piece of it, so I kept it."

"Good idea." Doug should have released it, but Bill was too distracted to care.

"What part do you think he'd like best?"

"Liver, I s'pose," Bill answered. "That's good for lots of things."

"Where is it?"

"Could find it in a rabbit all right."

"Yeah, who couldn't? But this is a fish."

"Oh, just give him anything." Bill handed over his sheath knife, and Doug opened the fish. "Phew!" He speared the trout on the point of the knife and tossed it disdainfully over his shoulder. "Even a crow couldn't eat that junk. It stinks. Let's go look for butterflies. Where's Jane's net?"

"Around."

"Well, get it."

Bill got slowly to his feet and shuffled to the toolshed. The net was in a corner with the hoe and a rake.

As the boys headed toward the garden, unpleasant thoughts of the night before goaded Bill's memory. He thought uncomfortably of his father's disobeyed summons. I couldn't very well leave Doug, he thought.

There weren't many butterflies. Bill didn't bother to do much looking.

"Give me the net, you dimwit. There's one right over here!" Excitedly Doug snatched the net and swooped it over a fluttering bit of white, jarring Bill's attention back to butterflies. He watched intently as Doug grabbed the wings through the gauze of the net. Then the shadow that fell over his shoulder, made him look up. Above him was the tall substance of the shadow. Behind his father's stern eyes was a worried sadness. Bill dropped his gaze from his father's face and let it follow his

81

father's pointing hand. His finger showed the way to Bill's footprint of the night before in the fine dirt of the bean field. Without speaking, his father turned and walked away.

Doug was too absorbed in the complications of feeding his bird to notice what went on over his head. Bill looked down without interest at the pink triangle formed by the wide open bill.

"Kim wants to see your kid."

"Let him," said Bill.

"You sure are in a green-apple mood. What's eating you anyway?"

"Nothing."

"Sure looks like something." Doug shook his head in disbelief. "Only two more weeks of school, then we got the whole summer with Deer Fly and Brighty." Doug was still wagging his head. "Anyhow, you're no fun. Guess I'll go see what's up with Kim."

Bill watched Doug go back toward the house. Shortly Bill heard the bike rattle down the driveway. For the rest of the morning he shuffled around the barn waiting for that talk with his father. It was going to be rough.

His mother called him to lunch. He didn't realize it was that late. Mostly he just pushed his food around his plate. When the meal was over, his father called Bill to him. They went outside, down the steps, and halfway across the yard before his father spoke. "Do you remember what I told you about Mr. Crawley the day after you saved Mr. Rutherford's dog?" He paused. Bill was silent. "I'm sure you do."

"Yeah." Bill's head was so low he seemed to be talking to his father's boots.

"I told you he was dangerous. I meant it. Guys like that can go haywire." His father paused, concern puckering his forehead in two lines up between his eyes. "Remember that half-starved cat you and Doug found in the Masons' chicken house?"

"Yeah. I remember all right. I've still got the scars."

"Mr. Crawley's like that cat. He's starved. And not only for food. He's starved for just about everything a man needs. Do you see what I'm trying to tell you?"

"Yeah, and I'm sorry I snuck out. I won't do it again, honest."

"I should hope not. Even a stupid rabbit has enough sense to guard its own life."

"Maybe that's 'cause rabbits don't get to wondering."

"Yes. Yes, I guess that's right. Rabbits don't get to wondering," he repeated as he turned and went slowly back to the field.

Bill stood in the middle of the yard puzzling over the conversation with his father. He hadn't been punished. He hadn't even been scolded, really. But Pa is worried, he thought. He thinks the Spook might do anything. Even kill.

Bill walked back to the house and into the kitchen. "Look out!" The warning came from his mother who was walking from the stove to the sink with a colander full of steaming asparagus. Bill watched her dump it into the sink bobbing with ice cubes. Because she was freezing asparagus, he could see that there would be no talking with her. "It would be a big help if you would label some of these boxes for me," she suggested.

Bill was restless. He just couldn't sit at the kitchen table. "Pa left that load of straw by the raspberries, so I s'pose I'd better go spread it." Quickly Bill melted backwards out of the kitchen before his mother had time to change the suggestion to a demand. He shuffled off in the direction of the garden. His leg ached a little after last night's running, and he didn't feel like hurrying.

The raspberry canes were beginning to leaf out, but only the first row had been trimmed and tied upright to stakes. In the other three rows the canes, some of them seven feet tall, were lying on the ground. Many of the wispy tops had winter killed. It was a depressing tangle surrounded by a yellow pile of straw bales. Halfheartedly he looked for the fork. Why had he told his mother he was going to spread that mountain of straw? He'd said it on an impulse. Maybe the fork wasn't there. He was about to turn away when he saw the handle sticking out of a bale on the side of the pile. With a sigh he took it in his hands and thrust it into the straw. Although the twine was broken, the bales still held their form, making it hard to pull the tight layers from the pile. Bill shed his windbreaker and threw it on the ground. Working's better than thinking, he thought as he thrust, carried, dumped, and thrust again. He laid the straw on nearly six inches deep where it would hold the moisture in the light silt loam and keep the sun from the sprouting weed seeds when they tried to grow. The decomposing straw would feed the earthworms. "In the raspberry patch, they're the only plows we need," his father had said. "The intestines of the soil you might call them."

Bill thrust again and was surprised to see that the pile was nearly gone. There was only enough for the first row, and that was lucky because it would take a long time to mulch the un-trimmed rows. The last forkful. Bill speared it with relief. As he lifted it from the ground, a whirling spiral caught his eye. The brown thing searched for cover in the scattering of straw left on the ground. It looked as though parasites were clinging. On closer examination, Bill recognized the pink jelly beans of baby mice gripping their mother's belly as she raced for her life. Then her darting circles found direction in her streak for the shelter of Bill's cast-off jacket. How can she run with all those babies dragging her back? he wondered. Perhaps one fell. Carefully his eye followed her path. Slowly he walked toward the jacket. A few feet away he stopped so as not to disturb her again. He saw no trace of a lost passenger.

Bill went to the spot behind the barn where Deer Fly was tethered. She was lying down, chewing her cud. "Hi, Kid. I saw a mouse. Boy, did I give her a scare. She was just as scared as I'd be if the Spook snuck up on me." A ball of cud came up Deer Fly's throat. The large eye so close to his was at once reflecting surface and deep as a well. Bill rested with his head pillowed against the kid's side.

The sun was getting low. Bill heard his father's voice and slowly got up to help with chores.

Chapter 10

Summer Begins

"Holy catfish, school's really out!" Doug stood on the shoulder of the county road with Bill, Jane, and Sammy, watching the orange tail of the school bus fade in a cloud of dust.

"Yippee!" shouted Sammy. Jane threw down her books and bent over in a backbend, her red pigtails brushing the gravel behind her.

Doug turned to Bill. "Gee! Your sister has a back like a wet noodle."

"Yeah," Bill agreed, feeling a pleasant surge of pride. "She does all right." Jane and Sammy ran toward home with the older boys following, deep in conversation.

"Never thought I'd make it," Doug said, proudly tapping a swelling in the vicinity of his stomach. A loud squawk advertised the presence of Brighty.

"You mean Miss Sorenson never did find out?"

"Oh, she found out all right, but not until the second week."

"What did she do then?" asked Bill.

"I told you before. Don't you hear anything these days? She let me keep him."

"How come?"

"She said, if it didn't disturb the class and if I kept up in my work, I could keep him. She let me give a report to the class on blue jays and everything."

"Sure hope I get her next year. Miss Brown is poison!"

"Say, how about coming down to the stream for awhile?" suggested Doug. "You haven't been down to my place for weeks."

"Yeah, that's a good idea," Bill said with some of his old enthusiasm. "But I gotta go home and drop all these books and get Deer Fly first."

"Do you have to take that goat everywhere?"

"Not to school," Bill said with a grin.

Doug laughed. "I'll walk home with you." After walking most of the way in silent thought, he turned to Bill. "Hey, listen to this:

> Billy had a Nanny goat,
> Her fleece was chocolate brown.
> In school she followed him about
> Which made the teacher frown.

Pretty good, eh?"

"Nice play, Shakespeare."

Deer Fly strained against her tether and bleated a loud welcome to the boys as they came laughing toward her. Bill unsnapped the chain and she followed, dancing at his heels, now and then pausing to nibble at an inviting twig or weed. Doug caught a grasshopper for Brighty. "See how his feathers are coming out?" he asked with pride.

"Yeah. Ma says it was smart of you to be able to raise him."

"It takes work all right, but now he doesn't have to eat all the time, so I can leave him in a cage if I want to. Kind of nice to have him along though."

"What did your mother do when she found out?"

"She said if he made a mess around the house, I'd have to get rid of him. I thought she'd be mad, but she kind of likes me to have him 'cause it gives her something to hold over my head."

"How come?"

"Now if she wants me to do something, she just says, 'Do it, or you can't keep Brighty.'"

"That sounds mighty low to me."

"Yeah. My parents do stuff like that, but they're not home much, so I can keep out of their way most of the time."

Deer Fly and Brighty sampled weeds and bugs from the cafeteria along the way, so progress was slow. After Doug dropped his books on his back porch, the boys walked through the yard and past the empty chicken house where Bill had been scratched by the wild, half-starved cat. "Too bad having all these buildings empty."

"Yeah," Doug agreed. "The whole thing seems sort of silly. Pa quit farming 'cause farming was too much work. Now just living is too much work. All he does is sit down and paint signs all day. When he gets home, he can't keep his eyes open in front of the TV. Wish he had some zip like your pa. He's always running."

"Oh, I don't know. Pa's always making me work."

"Yeah, I suppose that's a bad thing. But he's letting you off today, isn't he?"

"And tomorrow too. I work at Mr. Rutherford's in the morning though, but that's fun."

"You should kick!"

The boys reached the green fringe of poplar and willow that lined the stream bank. Doug took the pouch from his neck. "Phew! This sure needs cleaning." He held the hot little body of the jay in his hand and threw the makeshift nest on the ground. Doug looked at the bird and laughed. The cord of its neck stretched up to the open beak, and quilled flippers fanned the air.

Bill scratched at a lump behind his ear, then held out a little brown tick. "How do you think this would be?" he asked.

"Should be good. Put it in."

Bill coaxed the wood tick onto the tip of his finger, then thrust it down the peeping throat. "Say, did you ever notice those two little horns at the bottom of his tongue?"

"Yeah, funny aren't they? Sort of catch on to your finger. Now I'll put him in the hideout while I go to the stream and get some of that dead grass for his nest." Doug took Brighty to a gigantic maple guarded by an army of saplings. He gave a furtive look over his shoulder, like a spy about to pass into enemy territory. He slipped around the tree and disappeared into the hollow cavity on the far side. "Smells nice and moldy in here," he called out, his voice muffled.

"Be with you in a minute." There was just room for the two boys to squeeze into the hollow tree together, but it was too tight to stay long.

Bill came out of the hideout first and flopped on his stomach on the bank of the swollen stream with his head out over the water. "She's pretty high. I can drink from here." The wiry shelf of hair that grew out like a visor over Bill's eyes preceded his nose and mouth and pricked the water as he drank from the spring-fed stream.

"Hey, your beard's getting in the way," Doug joked.

"Yeah. Gotta get Pa to cut it."

"Say, I see why the water's high!" Doug exclaimed, pointing downstream.

Bill looked to a pile of sticks that lay heaped across the stream. "Beaver!"

"Maybe if we're real still, we'll see 'em."

It was so comfortable on the grass that they lay there for a long time. Bill went to sleep. When he opened his eyes, Doug was staring downstream. Bill lifted his head. As he did so, a dark shape at the head of a trailing *V* disappeared underwater and a re-sounding slap punctuated the retreat.

"You dope. You shouldn't have moved. You scared him."

"How was I to see with my face down there in the grass?"

"Anyhow he's gone. We might as well go home."

"Beaver sure do change things," Bill commented.

"Yeah. That dam'll make a neat place to swim this summer."

Doug collected his jay, gave it some chick starter, then they were on their way home.

"Kim got his new dog," Doug said.

"Oh?"

"Yeah, that bulldog he's always talking about. Kim wants to bring it over and show it tomorrow."

"I'll look at it, but I won't like it," Bill said with a grin.

"So long." Doug rolled under the loose-wired fence by the barn. "I'm going to stop off by the old manure pile. May find a few bugs in it for Brighty."

"See you tomorrow." Bill put a hand on Deer Fly's withers while they walked across the road toward home.

★ ★ ★

When Bill came back from Mr. Rutherford's Saturday morning, his father was walking—not running—from the barn toward the machine shed. He stopped under the elm when he saw Bill. "What plans for today?"

"Kim's coming over. Got a new dog. A bulldog Doug says."

"Sort of a portrait of his old man, eh?"

Bill laughed. "You said it."

"The bulldog used to be a real one: good legs and a strong jaw. People started using him for bull-fighting in the ring, and breeders got the idea that if they got his nose back out of the way, he could still breathe while he was hanging on to the bull's neck."

Sammy stopped playing with his truck and came over to join them. "Gee, that must've been something to watch," he said.

Their mother, on her way to take the breakfast leftovers to the chickens, turned to Sammy. "Not unless you like to see animals killed for sport. I think it's an awful idea."

"So do I," agreed Jane, who was on the back steps picking burs out of her butterfly net.

"Those crazy breeding practices have come home to roost."

"How, Pa?"

"The smashed-looking nose makes it hard for the dog to breathe. That causes respiratory infections."

"What's that?" asked Sammy.

"Colds. Then they bred great big heads so the dogs would have strong jaws. The heads got so big that some of the bitches couldn't have pups in the normal way and had to have caesarians." He turned toward Sammy. "That means they have to cut the females open to get the pups out, then sew them back up again. And all that for a deformed monster that's doomed to die in seven or eight years instead of the usual thirteen or fourteen years for a dog like Annie."

"Sounds crazy," Bill commented.

"It *is* crazy. And I've got to get back to work." He trotted on to the machine shed and was soon rolling toward the cornfield with the cultivator hitched behind his tractor.

It wasn't much later when Doug and Kim came into the yard. "Hey, Bill," Doug called.

Bill finished tying Deer Fly's new long rope to an apple tree in front of the house and, hands in pockets, strode to meet the boys. He stared hard at Kim. The taut leash was wound around his plump hand, holding back the brindle bulldog straining his bowed legs against the leash and wheezing his dissatisfaction with the restraint. "Dad imported him from England," Kim announced importantly. "He cost five hundred dollars."

That declaration had the desired effect. Bill's and Doug's jaws dropped. "All that money for a *dog*!" Doug exclaimed incredulously.

Kim explained. "His sire was the top-winning dog on the continent last season. His dam was almost as good. Dad figured we got a real bargain."

Bill was the first to recover from his astonishment. He leaned against the elm. With his hands still thrust deep in his pockets, his head tipped back, and his eyes half closed, he challenged, "What can he do?"

"We haven't had him long."

"Then I suppose about all he can do is come when he's called."

"Oh, he can do that all right. Dad just likes me to keep the leash on him 'cause he's such a valuable dog."

"Too bad. Thought I'd see something." Bill gave an ostentatious yawn and turned his back on Kim.

"Bet he won't even come when you call him," Doug jibed, turning after Bill.

"He will so!" With impulsive anger, Kim stooped and unsnapped the leash from the lunging beast. At the sudden release of tension, he almost toppled to his blunt nose. Then, just in time, he gathered his bowed legs under him and lumbered forward. After snuffling around the yard for a short time, he caught sight of Deer Fly tethered under the apple tree. The boys laughed as he took off in a series of rolling bounds.

"What's his name?" Doug asked, watching the clumsy animal with mingled amusement and contempt.

"Aspen Manor's Lord Drum is his registered name, but his call name is *Drum*."

Sammy had heard the boys and come up with Annie.

"You'd better call him," Bill said. "He's heading for Deer Fly."

The kid was regarding the strange monster cautiously, but without fear. Drum stopped and barked. Deer Fly took a couple of steps backward, then lowered her head. That slight semblance of retreat was enough to bolster the bulldog's courage. He lunged at Deer Fly as his ancestors had lunged at a charging bull. Deer Fly whirled her light frame and bounded round her tether like a deer pursued. Bill noted with alarm that she was winding her rope around the tree. Drum lumbered on, tongue lolling from the heavy head and nearly trailing on the ground. Only a few more circles before Deer Fly would be trapped and at the mercy of Drum's sharp teeth protruding from heavy jaws. Bill darted forward and intercepted Deer Fly a few feet from the tree. The rope was knotted to her collar. In her panic she wouldn't stand still to let him untie it. As she twisted and strained, Bill fumbled with the knot. "Call that dog," he shouted to Kim.

Drum ignored the call. His small, red-rimmed eyes were fixed on the helpless kid, while the easy-flowing saliva hung from his flews like honey. He crouched, his dark body curved over his short legs like the shell of a snapping turtle. Then, with a lunge he uncoiled, reaching for the neck of the little doe only two feet away. His teeth never found their hold. A level-running arrow of black and white stabbed the loose folds of skin over Drum's shoulder. Ponderously, the bulldog turned on his attacker. His jaws snapped empty air while the fleet collie left the marks of her teeth in his ear. Drum was no match for the lightning nipper, and no one knew it better than he. Soon Annie had him on his back squealing for mercy. With the innate sense of fair play born in most dogs, she refused to bite when he was down. Reluctantly she let her vanquished adversary run whining to his master.

By this time Bill had untied Deer Fly, who quickly found sanctuary on the top of the Brock's car. Annie was back at Sammy's side, her ears alert, her quick eyes watchful. Kim was attempting, with trembling hands, to snap the leash to Drum's collar.

Doug turned to Sammy. "You've got a mighty smart dog there. That sure was a piece of fast action!" he exclaimed.

"Annie takes care of things." The collie's action had been no surprise to the doting Sammy.

Bill wiped the sweat off his forehead with the back of his hand and moved away from the group to the far side of the car. He stood there for a moment or two, studying his goat. The nervous twitching of her tail and stamping of her hoofs had stopped. She seemed to realize the security of her perch. Bill turned his back on her. "Take a look, big man, and I'll give you your first lesson," he said to Kim, then whistled two short high notes. With relief, he heard the clang of hoof against metal as the goat sprang down to the hood, then thudded to the ground. Bill opened his mouth in a studied yawn, then without looking down, dropped his hands to Deer Fly's withers. "What was it you called me in the school bus that time last winter? A billy goat trainer? When you get your five-hundred-dollar dog as good as my goat, come on back, and I'll give you lesson number two."

Kim started home.

"Mighty smooth. Boy, that was some show," Doug congratulated.

"Some show-off, you mean." The taunt came from Jane who had been watching from the porch steps. "You shouldn't be so mean to Kim."

Doug went on, ignoring her. "Just you wait. It won't be long 'til my jay's just as good. In fact I think I could teach him a few things right now. Wish I'd brought him."

"Why don't you go back and get him?"

"Good idea. Think I will."

"I'll walk out to our mailbox with you." Bill tied Deer Fly before starting.

"You know," Doug said, "you should get your dad to help you train Deer Fly. Bet he knows a lot about it."

"Bet Mr. Rutherford knows even more. If I see him tomorrow morning, I'll ask. He's trained more dogs and horses even than Pa."

"Maybe he can help with Brighty, too."

"Maybe," Bill said doubtfully, "but birds aren't much like dogs and horses and goats." They had reached the mailbox, and Bill sat down to wait.

"Okay." Doug crossed the road at a trot.

Bill lay on his back and closed his eyes to the sun. The summer sounds kept his ears busy. A meadowlark called from across the road. He heard a mourning dove lamenting from a nearby telephone wire, and the guttural bubbling of a cowbird in the pasture. That was three. With his eyes closed, he counted three more: a friendly chickadee close over his head, the caw of a crow, and the clear note of a cardinal. Then he heard the alarm call of a jay, loud and insistent. "He must see Doug coming," Bill thought. With his eyes still closed, he listened for the footsteps. They were approaching heavily. Doug must be carrying the cage. The steps halted upwind of him, and the scent of manure blew strong to his nostrils. "Phew!" he exclaimed. "Where have you bee..." He opened his eyes. His voice failed him in the middle of the word. He flattened himself to the ground like a horned toad trying to make itself invisible. It was not Doug.

"Been waiting for me long?" the old Spook croaked.

Bill struggled to his feet. "I was waiting for somebody else." Old Man Crawley was close to him now. Bill could duck and run, but he checked the impulse when he remembered his father's advice. "How are you, Mr. Crawley?" he asked with a breathy voice.

"I been good. You better hurry on now."

Bill was relieved. "Yeah, I was just going," he said, and

quickly spun around. As he tensed his muscles to run, a clamp closed on his arm.

"You're headin' the wrong way, young fella."

There was no shaking that viselike grip. Bill felt weak as a wild cat without teeth or claws.

"School's out now, ain't it?" Bill nodded mutely. "Didn't your pa tell you?"

Still he couldn't speak. Never before had he been so close to the Spook. He could see the pores in his large nose like tiny wells of ink. The lines down from the corners of his mouth were brown and deep from the slow river of tobacco juice. "Come along, boy. We've got work to do."

"But I can't go yet. I've got to tell my friend where I'm going."

"You got to come *now*." His leer was intended as a smile, but the unused muscles of his face couldn't pull up the corners of his mouth. "He'll know you ain't here when he sees you gone." His rusty laugh grated against Bill's ears.

As Old Man Crawley pulled him along, Bill watched for a car that could mean a chance for escape, but the road was empty. Keeping a furtive silence, Crawley pulled him in quick jerks until they had come nearly to his rutted driveway. Suddenly Bill felt the grip on his arm tighten as the Spook tugged him toward the ditch with a fearful look behind him—at nothing Bill could see.

"What is it?" Bill asked. The Spook answered as an animal might, with a rolling in his throat. He pulled Bill off the highway to the track into his yard. "This is gonna be nice," he said. "Havin' a boy to help." Behind a tangled hedge of dying lilacs crowded by box elders, Bill was hidden from the road. He heard a car pass—out of sight.

"You're big now. You look strong." The words were pleasant enough, but not from the Spook. Bill felt like a bull being pushed into the ring to his death.

With the same firm grip on Bill's arm, Old Man Crawley

walked across the yard. Brush, weeds, cartons, and tin cans cluttered the path of trampled weeds. They passed next to the rotting carcass of a calf. Its stench pervaded the air. Bill saw a shovel leaning against a shed past the decomposing calf. Would he be asked to dig a grave for that putrid carcass? Bill tried to turn off his imagination, but all the death and injury farm life had shown him became pictures of his own fate.

"You pitch hay?" The sound, even the Spook's voice, was a relief from his thoughts. Bill nodded. The old man was leading him toward the house. "A hot day. I gotta get my hat," he said, opening the screen door and pushing Bill ahead of him. There was a jagged hole in the screen, and the swarm of flies on the calf carcass had free access to the house.

Old Man Crawley led Bill through the small dark kitchen buzzing with flies. They passed a rough cupboard, a table and chair, a wood stove, then stopped in front of the sink. There was no plumbing attached to it, and a pail under the drain caught the waste water. Bill noticed the entrails of a chicken floating in the slop pail. "Thirsty?" Crawley asked, taking a dipper from the water pail on the drainboard of the sink.

Bill thought of Blue retching up poison. He shook his head. "I'm not thirsty." He watched the water drip down the stubble of the old man's chin. He plunged the dipper back into the water pail, then crossed the room and took his hat from a nail near the door. The straw around the band was stained dark.

Suddenly, he jerked Bill toward him and crouched against the wall, apparently trembling with fear. Again Bill asked, "What is it?"

The Spook didn't answer but straightened up and pulled Bill across the kitchen to a door at the opposite side. For a moment he hesitated, then he turned the handle, and the door squeaked open. Yellow shades were pulled. The parlor smelled of dust and mildew. There was a picture on the wall, but its identity was hidden under dust. In the center of the room was a long plush couch laced with cobwebs. "There," said Crawley pointing a shaky finger, "right there she was laid out." Bill could imagine that she was still there. "Afore she dies, she says to me, 'Mel,' she says, 'I couldn't do nothing with you in my life, but I ain't a gonna stop after I'm dead.' And she didn't neither," the old man added with a rattle in his throat. "She's been a followin' me ever since, and sometimes when I turn quick, I see her eyes a lookin' at me, and a stick in her hand." He stood looking at the couch. His hand was cold and wet around Bill's arm. "Say... yeah, it was my hat I wanted." Although it was in his hand, he went to get it, pulling Bill after him. As he closed the parlor door, he looked stupidly at the hat in his hand. "Oh, yeah, I got it here," he said. They walked through the kitchen, their feet rustling the newspapers on the floor.

The old man closed the door behind them, then tugged Bill toward the machine shed. The checked boards of the wall let the light come through. The rusty hodgepodge of steel made the place look like a scrap-metal dump, and Bill found it difficult to distinguish a plow from a harrow in the confusion. An assortment of forks and shovels leaned against the wall in a corner. Crawley released Bill's arm and reached to pull a fork from the jumble of handles.

In an instant, Bill was running with the Spook's voice speeding him faster. "Run from your rightful work, will you? I'll get you yet. It's my rights."

* * *

Bill ran stumbling across the cloddy field toward his father's tractor. "Pa, Pa, did you tell the Spook I'd work for him?" Even though he knew the answer, he had to hear it from his father.

"Of course I said no such thing."

Bill told his father how the Spook had led him to his house, but he couldn't find the words to explain Crawley's mother.

"That man should be locked up. But if we tried and failed…" His father had been talking to himself, and two deep lines cut upward between his eyebrows. He looked at Bill and gave sharp orders. "Don't go near his place alone, and never leave home without telling your ma or me where you're going."

It would do no good to tell the rest, Bill thought. He'd only worry more. Bill walked toward the house. He thought about Crawley and the dead mother that haunted him, thoughts that didn't fit, that stretched and swelled in his brain until they hurt.

Chapter 11

Skunked

Bill had just returned from Mr. Rutherford's when Doug rode into the yard. His bike seemed to shake with anger. "Why did you sneak out on me yesterday?" he demanded.

"He had some work he wanted me to do."

"Well, of all the low-down dirty tricks. After your pa said you could have the day off. At least you could have told me."

"I wanted to, but he wouldn't let me." Although he was telling the truth, the words were as deceptive as a lie, and they made Bill feel just as uncomfortable. But it would be worse to spill the beans about Old Man Crawley.

"I'm glad you aren't giving me the brush-off. It's lucky for you you're not, 'cause I think I've found something really great down by the hideout."

"What is it?" Bill asked, grateful for the change of subject.

"If you follow me, I'll show you something to make your eyes pop."

It would be good to get away from the house, but the Spook might come back. He couldn't leave the kid. "Wait up. Just let me untie Deer Fly." Bill ran down the driveway and into the orchard in front of the house. In a few seconds he had freed the kid and was following Doug. He gave a furtive look down the road before crossing to the Masons' side. This time he was relieved to see no motion.

Doug was leading him in a circuitous path through the weed-grown pasture. "We gotta be careful," he hissed. "Kim's on the warpath. He's plenty mad about how we put it over on him yesterday. If we don't watch it, he'll find the hideout. I caught him snooping around our place yesterday."

"You don't say," Bill responded, trying not to let his voice show his indifference. Eluding Kim seemed childish.

Deer Fly and the boys came on the hollow tree from the downstream side and stealthily approached the moldering cavity. "Shh," Doug hissed as he slid sideways into the trunk.

"Say!" Bill exclaimed, surprised to see a stream of sunlight filtering through the upstream side of the tree. "How come the window?"

"Isn't it neat? I cut it yesterday after I left your place. Take a look out."

Bill put his eye to the three-inch window. "You sure get a dandy view of the bank. Say, there's a woodchuck hole, or something. Looks used."

"Yeah. That's the secret. It's used all right. I saw fresh tracks around it yesterday aft'. Then last night Ma had off, so she and Pa were both home. Boy, it was rough. I don't like to listen to their rows, so I snuck out and came down here. The moon was out so I could see pretty good. I kept a sharp lookout on that burrow until pretty soon, guess what walked out?"

"A woodchuck?"

"Wrong. Try again."

"Fox? No," Bill corrected, "the hole isn't big enough."

"Wrong again. Give up?"

"Yeah. What is it?"

"Skunks."

"You kidding?"

"Besides that, I bet they've got a family, and you know? I saw the funniest thing last night. One of them came out and snooped around for a while. It got right up to the tree, then I saw something jump. Looked like a frog or maybe a leaf that the wind hopped up, only there wasn't any wind. When the skunk jumped it and played with it, sort of like a cat with a mouse, I figured it must be a frog. He just rolled it around on the grass for a long time, then he carried it down into the hole. I kind of wondered what it was all about, so this morning I called Miss Sorenson."

"You called your teacher?" Bill asked incredulously.

"Yeah, she knows about things. She knew what it was too. She said skunks eat toads, but the warts over their eyes have a bitter milky stuff in them, so skunks roll them on the ground to squeeze the stuff out. Then they eat 'em."

"I'll be darned."

"Tell you what. There's an old shovel down by the beaver dam. Let's dig them out and catch the babies and raise 'em. They've got this operation to take the smell out of 'em. We can each have one and sell the others. They're real gentle, so just lots of people want 'em for pets, and we can get a pile of money."

"Sounds mighty smelly."

"Nope. I got that fixed. You know, there's one thing a skunk won't squirt at, and that's snakes."

"Did Miss Sorenson tell you that too?"

"No, this is something I've known all my life, only I never had a chance to try it before. All you do is get hold of a snake skin and wrap it around your hand. Then the skunk smells snake and won't let go at you."

"Have you got a skin?"

"I got a whole bunch of shed skins. Been saving 'em for an age."

"Then, I'll just step out of the way—way out of the way—and let you try it."

"First off I'm going to get the shovel." Doug ran to the stream with Bill following. Deer Fly bleated at the boys as they came out of the hollow, then bounded after them. It took some kicking around in the sticks and gravel beside the stream before Doug found the shovel. "Looks pretty rusty, but I guess she'll do the trick."

They hurried to the burrow. Under a young basswood the mound of orange-colored clay and gravel was conspicuous against the black topsoil. At their feet, the hole went down between two exposed roots. The boys looked at each other, fully aware of the strong defenses guarding the fortress.

"What are we waiting for?" Doug asked, plunging the shovel into the tough ground. He had to jump on it with both feet to get a start.

To Bill the progress was painfully slow. "You're taking it out in bird-beaks. Give me a crack at it."

"Okay, smart guy. You pile up the dirt for a while. And remember, that shovel wasn't born yesterday. I'll get the skins." Doug passed the shovel to Bill and took off toward his house.

Bill whittled away at the resistant dirt. "That skunk sure must be some digger," he muttered to Deer Fly. "S'pose some woodchuck dug it first. These roots are really rough!"

When he heard Doug coming back through the brush he shouted, "I'm down about a foot, and she's leveling out. It'll be a clear squirt from here." Bill put down the shovel and stepped back. "I've had it."

Doug carried a ball of string and a coffee can nearly full of snake skins he'd found in the grass, left where the snakes had slid out of them when they were outgrown. "Just help me tie these on, and I'll finish up," he said handing Bill the wispy skins.

"Something tells me *you'll* be finished up," Bill said as he awkwardly tried to hold the skins in place and wrap the string around Doug's hand at the same time. "This is like trying to hog-tie an octopus."

When the job was finally finished, Doug took a critical look at his hand. "Lucky it's dark in there, 'cause this sure doesn't *look* like a snake." Doug gave his hand a sniff. "Lucky skunks have better noses than mine. I can't smell a thing."

"You'll smell plenty when you're through. Bet you fifty cents you come out smelling worse than the Spook."

"Shake on it." Doug held out his snake-gloved hand. "Careful," he warned as Bill was about to take it. "These things are mighty delicate." Bill shook as though with a butterfly's wing, and the deal was made.

"You don't seem to be in any hurry," Bill observed.

"I'm not worried. It's just that what you said about the Crawling Spook reminded me of something."

"I'll bet!"

"Honest. On the way up to your place yesterday, Kim told me Mr. Rutherford was missing a calf."

"Rustlers maybe," Bill said with a grin.

"I think it was the Spook, that's what I think."

Bill nodded. The dead calf he'd seen at old man Crawley's was real young and runty. Not even worth butchering. Maybe he'd tried to replace it with a good one from Mr. Rutherford's herd. It was hard to keep it all in while Doug rattled on not knowing the half of it.

"You know what we could do?" Doug went on. "We could go over to the Crawley place and do a little snooping."

Bill's secret was making his life harder and harder. "It sure would be nice to do something for Mr. Rutherford sometime," he said vaguely. "He's sure been great to us."

"I'd just love to pin something on the Spook." Doug picked up the shovel, then looked down at his hand. "Say, I can't dig with this stuff on."

With resignation Bill took the shovel. "So I get the pleasure." He jabbed at the tough roots until he found free dirt between one of them and the side of the burrow. He managed to enlarge the entrance considerably before running into another root. Bracing the shovel against the side of the burrow, he jerked. With a snap, the handle broke.

Bill stepped back and turned to Doug, who flopped on his stomach with a sort of growl and reached into the hole. Bill saw his legs convulse expressively before, a second later, the air was choked with skunk fumes.

Bill held his sides and laughed at the agonized gyrations of Doug's legs. He wriggled, snakelike, until his head and shoulders were free of the entrance, then stood erect and gasped for air. "It didn't work, but I got one," he choked out.

"You've got the old battle-ax herself. We don't want her!"

Doug, his eyes tightly closed, flung the black-and-white fur piece into a dense growth of brush and wild grape around a basswood tree. As the skunk hit the ground, there was a crashing through the vines. "Too heavy for a skunk," Bill muttered, looking up.

The boys listened, and for some time could follow the stumbling progress through the brush. "Kim!" Doug exclaimed. "He must know everything!"

"Hey, what's this?" Bill walked forward where, half hidden by brush, he saw a tin can with a trail of crinkle-headed morel mushrooms spilling from it.

"Kim must have been after mushrooms, but it doesn't make any difference. Even if he wasn't spying on purpose, he still knows everything."

"Yeah," Bill said doubtfully. Kim hunting morels? Now was no time to speculate. Doug sure was a sorry sight. "You look like you've been standing on your head in the honey pot." Bill held his nose. "But you sure don't smell like it!"

"All that, and not even one baby. By this time they should

have their eyes open and be real cute, but I didn't feel a one. Did you see any get out?"

"No. But after that guy went crashing through the brush, I wasn't looking." Picking mushrooms—funny thing for Kim to be doing, Bill mused. How would he know how to pick a time when the lilacs are in bloom, then go out after a rain and look under a basswood?

Doug was focused on his foiled plan and his present predicament. "Bet it would have worked if only I'd just had a fresh skin. No scent left on these."

"Want to make it another fifty cents?" Bill goaded.

"Shut up!" Doug exclaimed as he gyrated in agony. "I can't open my eyes. Boy this stuff is rough! Must have got some in my eyes, and it stings like crazy." He reached out in blind groping. "Help me down to the stream, will you?"

"If you don't mind, I'll keep my distance."

"A fine pal you are."

Bill took pity on his friend and searched for a way to help Doug from a safe distance. "Hold on. I'm helping you. Here. If you take the end of this handle, I can lead you to the water, blind man." Slowly Bill guided the tight-eyed Doug toward the shore with the broken shovel handle. "Well, here you are. Shed your stinky stuff while I go up to your place and get you some clean clothes."

"Okay. And get some soap too."

"I sure will."

Bill trotted along the streambed and through the Masons' pasture. He found the house empty, but after a little rummaging around he located everything he needed and returned to the stream.

"What took you so long?" Doug asked.

"Took a while to find everything. I brought you some nifty shampoo."

"What! Not that smelly stuff of Ma's!"

"Some of it may be hers. Here." Bill handed Doug a jar of harmless looking liquid.

Doug took a skeptical look, then smelled it. "What in blazes is it?"

"It's sort of a mixture I brewed up. Bleach and kerosene and cleaning fluid, and some shampoo to finish it off pretty."

"What you want to do? Take my hair off?"

"It's no good to you the way it is. That's a cinch. I brought you a bar of laundry soap for the finishing touches."

"Anyhow nobody can call me a sissy," Doug said tipping his head back and pouring the "shampoo" over his hair. He gave it a quick rub, then plunged under the water.

Doug was yelling and splashing in the icy water. It was dull, just watching. Bill swayed from one foot to the other and swung his arms forward and back in unison. "If you hadn't gone and stunk up the water, I might join you," he called over the stream. But Doug was swimming, and Bill's words were drowned before they reached his submerged ears.

After a quick look over his shoulder, Bill pulled off his T-shirt, then started to unbuckle his belt. Deer Fly trotted up and chewed at the end of the leather. Bill rubbed her forehead, then ran his fingers down the bumps of her vertebrae. "How about a swim, Kid?" She rubbed her head vigorously against his side, making Bill stagger a step or two sideways. "Find some other rubbing post, will you?"

Bill was soon splashing with Doug and laughing over their adventure. But the spring water was so cold they soon ran for their clothes.

Bill was struggling in an attempt to pull his T-shirt over his wet body. Doug was laughing at him. "You know what you look like?"

Bill's mutterings didn't make their way through his shirt.

"Like a python trying to get into a garter snake's skin."

"You should talk about snake skins!" Bill exclaimed, his red face emerging from the neck of the shirt just in time to see Doug worming his way into his pants with violent thrusts of his hips, like a disturbed caterpillar. Both of them laughed a long time, rolling in the sand, before their stomachs told them it was time to head for home.

As Bill walked, his hand on Deer Fly's withers, the laughter drained from him like water through sand. He thought uneasily of those crashing steps through the brush and tried to convince himself it was just Kim. With the happenings of yesterday fresh in his mind, everything he couldn't see and understand sharpened the point of his fear.

"So long."

Even Doug's friendly voice made Bill jump. "You going home now?" he asked, disappointed, even though he had scarcely been aware of Doug's presence as they walked from the stream.

"I'm just going to stop off and pick up Brighty and maybe get something to eat. I'll be over this aft'. When Mr. Rutherford comes home, maybe we can go down and see if he'll help train Brighty and Deer Fly."

"Okay, and don't forget my fifty cents. Even the Spook doesn't smell like you. See you later."

Bill walked along the county road, his eyes on the dusty puff kicked up by the toe of his boot. His gaze snapped into focus as his boot came heavily to rest on the sandy dome of an anthill. Bill watched the hysterical specks that had not been ground to death under his boot. The orange beads threaded with controls were following their waving antennae in circles to nowhere. As he lifted his foot, Bill felt his own vulnerability—as helpless as an insect. With empathy Bill surveyed the chaos he had created in the tiny community.

The large fuzzy leaves of a mullein grew at the side of the

road. He picked one and with it scooped up a few of the scurrying ants. "How about a new home?" he asked, careful not to blow his small refugees off the leaf with the wind of his voice. A few steps farther on he came upon another colony like the first. One sharp shake and the leaf riders fell to their new home. Bill watched in dismay as his ants were greeted by an army of warriors armed with deadly sickles. The annihilation was quick and complete.

Bill looked down the road with senses keen as a deer's.

Even on his own driveway he didn't feel safe. Although he walked toward the farmyard, his fears raced across the open like a rabbit seeking the security of a brush pile. As he stood at the corner of the barn, he noticed Annie in the pasture with the herd. He couldn't see what she was doing there, but it didn't matter. He turned away with a shrug. If he thought of it, he'd ask his father about it at lunch. The rumbling in his stomach told him it must be nearly time.

When he got into the kitchen, his father was already sitting at the table. "How come Annie's out with the cows?" Bill asked.

"The herd was ganging up on our new Holstein that was trucked in today, so I sent Annie out to stand guard. The others will soon accept her, and that will be the end of it."

"How come a herd will gang up on a strange cow?"

Bill's father paused a long time before answering. "That sounds like a simple question, but it's not," he said. "I can only give you part of an answer. Cows have a set social order with one old cow the leader. A new one has no place in the system. Until she makes a place for herself, the others will buck her." He paused, then continued. "But what's the gimmick in their makeup that makes them act like that? That's the real question, and I can't answer it. No one yet has been able to fathom all the ins and outs of a cow's brain. Maybe some day they will. Then you'll have your answer."

Bill's mother poured the last glass of milk and sat down with them. "Boys in school act just about the same way toward a new boy," she said.

"Ants kill a strange one. And quick."

His father looked up from his plate with a lively interest. "I didn't know that." Bill heard respect in his voice.

"They do. I saw it happen this afternoon." Bill told his story, and the simple facts sounded unimportant. Just a few dead ants, and who could think it mattered?

"Caterpillars wouldn't do a thing like that," said Jane.

"I wonder how the ants can tell a stranger," Bill's father mused.

"Cows fight a sick one, too," Sammy put in. "When the Cummings had one down with a heart attack or something, the others wouldn't let it get up. Why wouldn't they, Pa?"

"Animals just don't like weaklings. If there's something wrong with one of its kind, a lot of animals will either kill it or drive it out of the group."

"I suppose a cow feels that there's something funny-like when another cow is sick. Just not right. Sort of like the way we feel about Mr. Crawley." That name was always near the surface of Bill's thoughts, nonetheless it made him uncomfortable to hear it creeping out.

Mrs. Brock stood by the table, her hands full of plates. "You boys aren't so different. In your class who do you put at the bottom?" She answered her own question. "Kim, just because he's not like you and Doug."

"Yeah," his father pushed his chair back from the table. "We humans get our own pecking order for a lot of different reasons. Just two-legged animals. But now I've got to quit this discussion and get back to work."

Chapter 12

Training

As he walked across the yard, Bill almost wished his father had not given him two free days with time—too much time—to think. Ever since he had been old enough to look, Bill had seen birth and death, like seasons, thawing in spring, freezing in winter. Now it was different. Death felt close, like an icy armor. The day was hot, but he shivered.

Deer Fly saw him and bleated her welcome. Bill hurried toward her, glad to have a destination. "Hi there, Kid. Lonesome?" She rotated her ears to funnel in the sound of his voice. "Yeah, I know. I get lonesome too. Now with all this Spook business, I can't just say things out to anyone but you."

The kid lay in the grass, content with the nearness of the animal that fed her: a doe or a human, it made no difference to her. Bill sat beside her resting his head against her sun-warmed shoulder. As he talked to her, he could hear, or feel (he wasn't sure which) the beat of her heart. "Do you ever think about dying?" The young goat flicked her too-short tail at a buzzing fly, and Bill went on. "You were real scared that time Kim's dog went after you, remember?" The small jaw rotated on the cud, and lids dropped over her large eyes. Bill looked at the length of white eyelash and smiled. "You sure aren't much of a worrier. Let's you wake up, and we'll go take a look at the new cow."

The two walked to the pasture fence where Bill stepped down the bottom wire and held up the next strand for the kid. She hopped through like a dog with Bill behind her. He was barefoot, so the soft grass tickled the bottoms of his feet. With pride he noticed the almost complete absence of weeds in the pasture. His father had taught him to drive the tractor as soon as his legs were long enough to reach the brake and accelerator peddles. He had mowed the pasture last summer before seed pods had formed on the weeds. The green carpet looked almost like a lawn—except for the cow pies. The kid popped into the air, lit on her little hoofs and danced back to Bill. He caught her burst of life. With something close to the kid's lightness, he jumped and ran toward the cattle grazing in the distance. The feeling passed quickly; he slowed to a walk.

The black and white of the new Holstein stood out sharply from the white and tawny of the Guernseys. Bill marveled at the size of her udder and the capacity of the great barrel that contained the four compartments of her stomach. For a time he watched the tongue wrap the grass and pull it between her tearing teeth. The milk-making machine stuck to her task, boring Bill with the monotonous motion. As he started back, he noticed Annie stretched under an elm, alert but motionless. "You're a funny dog, not even coming to meet me." As he turned his back on the quiet guard, he noticed a curious heifer approaching the equally curious Deer Fly. The animals approached each other with cautious steps. Soon a small bevy of young Guernseys had gathered behind the lead heifer and were bearing down on Deer Fly with steady steps. As Bill watched, Annie darted in front of the advancing line and turned them back to the herd. "Spoilsport," Bill called after her in irritation. "I wanted to see what Deer Fly would do." Annie was back under her tree where Bill's

112

words didn't concern her. "I got to admit you're a good dog though." As he spoke, Annie's ears rose, then she let out a volley of barks. When he followed her gaze, Bill noticed two men walking through the Cummings' pasture toward him. They were still far away when they turned south heading for the Crawley place. Wonder what they're doing, Bill thought. Maybe something to do with Mr. Rutherford's stolen calf.

Bill was going under the fence, leaving the pasture, when he heard Doug's bike rattle into the yard. "What took you so long?" Bill called.

"Come here and see."

Bill walked over to him, first puzzled by what he saw, then amused. "You look like a hunchback hind side front."

"It's my new cage. See? Isn't it neat?" Doug parted his shirt, exposing a small birdcage hung around his neck on a length of binder twine.

"Yeah, that's quite a deal. How'd you make it?"

"I just used the top of a big can. See?" He stepped off his bike, which clattered to the ground, then took the contraption from his neck. "Then I took baling wire and put it through holes poked in the bottom and wired them all together on top. Now I don't have to lug that heavy cage."

"Should think the pouch would be easier."

"Brighty's no baby any more. He wants to stretch his wings. That old pouch'd just about crush him. This gives him a lot of freedom."

Bill regarded the fluffy clump of feathers. The baby shape was unkempt and irregular, a far cry from the sleek brilliance of its parents. As the cage tilted, Brighty reached out feathered arms to grab the air and with some difficulty maintained his equilibrium. "Looks about ready to fly," Bill commented.

"Yeah. Got any place where we could try him out?"

"The barn should be good."

The boys were soon in the loft. "This binder twine sure is scratchy," Doug complained, rubbing the chafed line on the back of his neck where the weight of the cage had rested.

Deer Fly bleated, her forefeet on the second rung of the ladder the boys had climbed. "I'll hoist her back legs, and you catch her by the shoulders when I get her up," Bill suggested, going back down the ladder.

"Do you have to bring her every place?"

"She wants to come," Bill said, pushing. They soon had her with them. She shook herself, then gave the floor a couple of rapid taps with her forefoot.

"Let Brighty out of the cage. I'll call him and feed him when he comes to me, okay?"

"Yeah, but how do you open the cage?" Bill asked.

"Just untwist the wires at the top."

Bill twisted and grunted as the wires dug into his fingers, then Brighty was free. Ever hungry, he peeped excitedly, beak gaping; he seemed to feel that he was too young to chase his own food. Doug came nearly to him, then, by holding a tempting glob of chick starter a little way from him, persuaded Brighty to hop a few steps. He still opened his beak like a baby, quivering his wings and swallowing Doug's finger along with the food as he uttered gulping peeps. Doug laughed. "Pretty good for the first lesson."

"Yeah, neat going," agreed Bill.

"Now let's see if he'll fly." Bill carried the bird back in his cupped hands and held him on Deer Fly's withers. Doug whistled again, and Bill released the bird, giving him a little push. He fluttered awkwardly to the ground, and after a few fruitless peeps for service, hopped to Doug's hand.

"Boy, does he learn fast!"

"Sure does."

As the afternoon wore on, Brighty flapped his way over longer and longer distances to fill his crop.

"Say," Doug said abruptly, "it must be about time to go to Rutherford's.

"Yeah, he should be getting home pretty soon."

"Wish Brighty wasn't so full. I'd sure like to show Mr. Rutherford how he comes."

The two boys and the two animals trudged south on the county road. As they approached the Crawley place, a whiff of skunk reminded Bill of his bet. "What about that fifty cents you owe me?"

"I haven't got it now. I'll have to get it out of Pa or else sell something."

"I ought to have guessed it. You know, I don't think you took much of a bath. It's smelling real powerful." Bill stopped. They were opposite the Crawley place. He saw on the corner post of the corral a flapping denim jacket. Bill's nostrils pinched as the south wind combed the folds of cloth and blew a load of skunk to his face. "It wasn't Kim!"

"What do you mean?" asked Doug, wrinkling up his nose.

"That crashing through the underbrush. It wasn't Kim. It was the Spook."

"Gee. He must have heard us talk about Mr. Rutherford's calf and how stinky he was and everything." Doug switched from dismay to cheerfulness. "Come to think of it, I don't owe you fifty cents. You owe me. Neat switch, isn't it?"

"I don't get it. You still got skunked."

"Yeah, but you bet I'd smell worse than Old Man Crawley, remember?"

"Guess you got me," Bill admitted. "It's kind of funny. But that means we'll have to call off our search. He'll be laying for us sure."

"Yeah."

Mr. Rutherford had not yet come home when the boys stopped by the pasture gate. "Look at that baby would you!" Doug exclaimed, pointing to the mares at the far end of the pasture. "I didn't even know she'd foaled."

Bill's thoughts were on Crawley. "I saw a couple of men going to the Spook's place earlier this aft'. At least I think that's where they were going."

"Did you?" Doug was absorbed in the foal. "Let's go take a closer look."

The mares raised their heads and regarded the boys doubtfully. It wasn't yet time for their grain. After the first inquisitive glance, they lowered their heads and returned to their grazing. Pheasant's baby was hard to see, just a small sorrel body poised on long knobby legs. No markings showed from where they stood.

"I'll stay here. I've seen her."

"Okay. Have it your way." Doug climbed the gate and ran toward the horses.

When Mr. Rutherford's car drove into the yard, Bill was looking out across the pasture. As the motor slowed behind him, he felt a wave of apprehension, even though he knew it was irrational to think it could be the Spook.

Mr. Rutherford closed the garage door. He saw Doug far out in the pasture, then carefully regarded Bill and his pet. "Deer Fly looks strong and sleek," he said. "I'm glad to see you both."

"Yes, she's fine." They shook hands.

Doug had seen the car drive in and was running back across the pasture. "Hello," he shouted. "Bill tell you why we came?" He stopped, breathless, at the gate.

"Not yet."

"We wanted to know if you'd help us train Brighty and Deer Fly. Can you?"

"I can't be certain so quickly. May I ask who Brighty is?"

"I thought you knew," Doug answered, taking the cage from around his neck and holding it out to Mr. Rutheford.

"He's a fine-looking young bird. You keep him nice and clean."

Doug glowed with the praise. "He has a bath every day right after breakfast."

"How old was he when you took him?"

"He was an egg." An egg, and now this chirping ball of feathers. Doug almost shared the doubt he saw on Mr. Rutherford's face, then he saw how it was and felt the egg in his hand. "It really happened. I saved it from a snake, then it hatched right in my hand."

Mr. Rutherford looked questioningly at Bill, who nodded. "I was there."

"It's not difficult to raise a blue jay when it's taken from the nest just before it learns to fly, but it's quite a feat to raise it from an egg. Now then, what do you want to teach these animals?"

"Tricks," Doug retorted promptly.

"And you, Bill?"

"I don't really know just what. I thought I'd ask you about it."

"I'll start by asking you some questions. Every boy wants a trained pet, but very few have enough knowledge and persistence to train one. Are you sure you want to undertake this?"

"We do," Doug stated quickly.

"First you must understand your animals. What are Brighty's most outstanding natural abilities?"

Doug looked intently at Brighty before answering. "He eats, and now he's beginning to fly."

"How can you turn those traits to tricks?"

Doug hung his head. It was clear he thought his first answer was silly. "I guess I can't."

"On the contrary. Those are the two most important things

you can use in training. Probably the first trick you will try to teach Brighty will be to fly to you for food."

"That's just what I was doing this afternoon!"

"Yes, and when your bird has learned that well and his wings are strong, you will see other traits as you study his actions. Then you can teach him more. Now Bill, how about you? What do you know about your goat?"

"She follows me, and she comes when I call her already, and she likes to jump up on things. And she likes to butt, too."

"You have a lot to work with." Mr. Rutheford gazed intently at Deer Fly, then at Brighty. "Both of you boys have done the groundwork well. You took your animals when they were young and shifted their allegiance from their own kind to you. But remember this. You are the ones who must understand how they think and feel, because they can never understand human thoughts and feelings. Study your animals. When you come back again, you should know what they are capable of learning."

"I know what I want to teach Deer Fly," Bill said quietly. "I want to teach her to climb a ladder and pull a cart."

"Yes, that shouldn't be too difficult. But I can't tell you just how to do it without knowing more about your goat. You said she likes to jump and climb. Does she ever do it when she is frightened or stimulated in some other way?"

"She jumped up on the car when she got loose after Kim's dog went after her."

"You may be able to put that experience to work. Next time you come, we'll get a ladder with wide steps and set it up in the riding ring. I'll let Blue out, and he'll probably bark at Deer Fly. If she goes even part way up the ladder, you give the command to climb. When you work at home you can offer something she likes to eat part way up the ladder, and she'll probably go up on her hind legs the first time you try it. But after that it will take many repetitions with you saying the commands as she climbs.

Eventually she'll associate the command with climbing, then, if you give the command before she climbs, she'll climb in response to the command. Then she will be reliable. Now, I want to give Blue a walk, so I'll go part way home with you."

The boys waited in the yard while Mr. Rutherford went into the house to get Blue. "Gee but he knows a lot!" Doug exclaimed. "Wonder how he found out so much about goats and birds. They aren't so much like horses. At least birds arcn't."

A quiet word brought Blue to heel, and he walked beside Mr. Rutherford trembling with eagerness to investigate the goat. The boys marveled at the strength of the invisible leash between man and dog.

"Mr. Crawley seems to have a skunk for company," Mr. Rutherford observed.

"No. That's not it. He got skunked down by the stream near our place. He was picking mushrooms." Doug went on to fill in the details while Mr. Rutherford exchanged glances with Bill.

Doug finished his story, then walked ahead. Bill was shuffling along the shoulder watching puffs of dust as he had that morning. He saw hills of industrious ants. Deer Fly's cloven hoof stepped neatly in the center of a large one Bill had walked around. He pulled the kid's collar, but too late. Mr. Rutherford was silently watching.

"We kill something with our feet most every step we take, don't we?" Bill asked.

"Yes, that's true," Mr. Rutherford agreed.

"Somehow it doesn't seem very nice. I wouldn't like to be stepped on."

"You aren't an insect, Bill."

"But nothing wants to die. I don't want to die."

"Everything living is in danger of dying, and of course you will die, someday. But not soon. Bill, remember: Fear accomplishes nothing. It will only blind your reason and hinder sensible action. Understanding and right actions can conquer your fear and make it helpless as a hog-tied steer." Mr. Rutherford put a hand on Bill's shoulder and smiled.

Doug had already passed the Brocks' mailbox. "So long," he shouted back, "and thanks."

"Good-bye, Doug," Mr. Rutherford called back. To Bill he said, "Good-bye, and remember. Treat your fear the way you treat your goat. Understand it, then tame it."

As he walked toward the house, Bill found himself imagining that Mr. Rutherford had supernatural powers that pulled secrets out of men and animals alike.

Chapter 13

Hand Fed

"Hey, look," Doug shouted. "See what I got?"

"You haven't got it yet." Bill watched Doug stalking his prey in the weedy grass at the edge of the lawn. Brighty, now almost streamlined with maturity, hopped near Doug's right hand, intently watching its every move. His head was cocked over his vivid body, blue set off with black markings and little snowballs tossed over his wings. Doug's hand stalked a green grasshopper taking its ease on a leaf of ragweed. Brighty saw it too, and his crested head bent toward the hopper in an ecstasy of anticipation. Doug's hand stopped moving as he fastened his eyes on the jay. Brighty's beak approached ever nearer until, suddenly, the grasshopper took off, letting fly with its hind legs. It kicked Brighty squarely under his eye. The startled bird fluttered backward.

"Just like I'd feel if a hamburger stood up and punched me," Doug roared. "Poor Brighty. I'll find you one without a temper." He soon had another grasshopper, causing the bird to open his beak like a nestling for Doug to pass it down his throat.

"Isn't he ever going to grow up?" Bill asked.

"I like him this way," Doug retorted. "If he got his own food, how would I ever train him? You can push Deer Fly around to show him what you want, but I can't push a bird in the air. Mr. Rutherford said I couldn't teach him anything unless he was hungry for a reward."

"Yeah, I know, but it looks mighty funny to see a grown bird open his beak like a baby."

"It's about time to go to Mr. Rutherford's, isn't it?"

"Must be."

The boys walked down the road as they had nearly every evening for a month. "Deer Fly climbs like anything now, so I'm going to start teaching her to pull pretty soon. Sure wish I had a cart."

"Brighty almost always comes when I whistle, and I can't wait to show Mr. Rutherford how he plays dentist."

As they passed the weathered buildings of the Crawley place, Bill glanced, as always, for movement in the yard. As usual, there was none.

"Mr. Rutherford never pinned that calf on the Spook, did he?" Doug asked.

"Naw. He would have got rid of it after he heard us talking down by the stream. Maybe he butchered it. Too bad with such good bloodlines. It was a heifer, so I bet he wanted to keep it for breeding."

A boy and a dog turned into Mr. Rutherford's drive, ending talk about the calf. The boys hurried on, curious to see who it was.

"I'll be!" Doug exclaimed. "It's Kim with Drum."

Doug and Bill stepped up in time to hear Kim say, "Pa says to give you this if you'll help me train him." He was holding money in his fist.

"No, Kim. It's not your father's money I want, but if you'll help me with the work, trimming the shrubbery perhaps, I should be very grateful."

"I think my dad would rather have you take the money. My summer's filled up with camp and stuff."

"Put it in your pocket, Kim." No matter how gentle his voice, Mr. Rutherford always seemed to command. It looked to Bill as though his mustache twitched as he spoke.

Doug leaned against the paddock fence, the jay on his head. Bill stood beside him, his hand on Deer Fly's neck. Kim waited uneasily in front of Mr. Rutherford. "But my father said..."

"What do you want to teach your dog to do?"

"Come when I call him and stuff like that."

"Why doesn't your dog obey you?"

"He's just spoiled, that's all. He wants everything his own way, and he figures he can get away with it."

"What do you do when you want him to come to you?"

"I just call him, but mostly he doesn't come."

"What do you do then?"

"I go after him."

"Can you run as fast as he can?"

"No, but..."

"But you have a game of tag, and your young dog enjoys it thoroughly, and when you catch him, if you do, do you scold him?"

"I give him a licking, and still he runs away."

Mr. Rutherford shook his head. "Would you go running to your father if always in the past when he had said the word 'come,' it meant a chase, and if he caught you, a beating? To your dog the word 'come' means 'run for your life.' Never use it again." Kim opened his mouth, then closed it. "Give me the leash, and I'll show you how it's done. What's your dog's name?" he asked as he took it.

"Aspen Manor's Lord Drum."

"The call name is enough."

"Drum."

"That's a good quick name. Now watch what I do." Mr. Rutherford straightened up and seemed about ready to call the dog, but instead he squatted on his heels. "You've got the chain collar on backwards." He showed Kim how to put it on so that the chain would slide freely through the ring, then stood up. "Drum." He spoke sharply to get the dog's attention, and when the head swung toward him, he called more gently, "Here, Drum. Here." Drum blinked his little eyes and stared. Mr. Rutherford repeated the command and jerked sharply on the leash. The bulldog braced his feet and pulled and wheezed. Suddenly the trainer released the tension on the leash, and the heavy dog fell backward to his haunches. Before he had a chance to gather his legs under him, Mr. Rutherford jerked him strongly forward, then reached out his hand to pat and praise him. As he spoke to the dog and stroked his head, he continued to step backwards calling, "Here," from time to time. The young dog followed amiably.

Mr. Rutherford straightened up. "Never allow your dog to go on a tight leash. Whenever he strains, jerk him as hard as necessary to make him give ground, then immediately let the leash go slack. When he walks close to your side, pat him and speak kindly to him. It may take you as long as a week to teach him that it's more pleasant to obey." He spoke with half his attention on the dog, working the leash at frequent intervals to keep the animal under control. He handed Kim the leash. "Now take him home and work with him a little every day. It will be easier to get his attention when he isn't distracted by strangers—especially a goat!"

Kim and Drum started battling their way down the road, the boy swearing as he jerked.

"And remember," Mr. Rutherford's voice stopped him. "You will never control a dog if you don't control yourself."

"He sure is making a mess of things, isn't he?" Doug commented.

"He isn't old enough to train," the old man said.

"What! He's as old as I am," Doug exclaimed.

"Age is not entirely a matter of years. Kim's like that jay of yours. He depends on his father's handouts, and he doesn't want it any other way. He wants to get things easily, and that dog will not be easily trained."

"Mr. Rutherford, I found out something," Doug exploded. "When Brighty isn't very hungry, he comes anyway—sometimes—when I give him something bright like a little piece of tin. He just flics away with it, but I thought maybe there'd be some way to teach him to bring it back, like a retriever."

"There may well be, but I think you'll have to find an enclosed space to work in. If you can find a place where you are the only perch, he may very well bring the object back to you. Then you can give him a bit of food. It should work, but I doubt very much if you could teach it to him in the open.

"Now, how is Deer Fly coming? You must be nearly ready to teach her to pull."

"That's just what I was going to ask you about. I've got the harness ready, but no cart. Maybe I can start her pulling a log or something."

"Fine. It's too late to start now, but next time you come, bring the harness with you." He walked toward the kennel. "I'll get Blue, and we'll walk to your house."

Mr. Rutherford always walked home with the boys. Doug didn't seem to think it strange, but Bill knew why he did it.

When Bill walked into the yard, Jane was in the orchard, white cloth fluttering from her hand. "What *are* you doing?" he asked.

"Fitting a sleeve on this apple tree, of course."

"Just why the fancy new clothes for an apple tree? Is it going to a party or what?"

Jane laughed. "Come here, and I'll show you." Bill walked

125

over to where Jane was slipping a tube of cheesecloth over a leafy branch. "First I tie it around the bottom end. Here, hold it for me while I pull the string tight. There." Jane stooped to pick up a jar.

"Now I get it. Say, they're kind of pretty." Bill examined the plump green caterpillars with red, yellow, and blue tubercles standing in rows down their backs like toy soldiers.

"Now you dump them in and tie up the top."

"Is that it?"

"Yup. When they eat all the leaves on this branch, I just move the sleeve. Neat, huh?"

"Did Pa say it was all right to let 'em eat all the leaves off the apple tree?"

"I can't put 'em anywhere else. I found 'em on apple, and they don't like to change food plants. Anyway they won't eat all the leaves. There're only ten."

"Okay. It's a good idea, keeping track of 'em and protecting 'em from birds." Bill turned to go.

"Wait up. Hold the top for me before you go."

"There," said Jane when she had tied the caterpillars inside, "Doesn't that look neat?"

"I don't know. Craziest dinner party I ever saw."

* * *

Two days later Bill was going out to the orchard to move Deer Fly's stake when he heard a moan from Jane. "They're gone. Every one." The cheesecloth was unraveling from a long rip.

Brighty sat on an upper branch of the apple tree, a caterpillar hanging from the corner of his beak like a fat green cigar.

Chapter 14

Strange Baits

"Oh Bil—ly," his mother called. "Are you going to Mr. Rutherford's to help your father with haying?"

Bill answered from the yard as he was coming back to the house after watering Deer Fly and moving her stake. "Yeah. We're going as soon as Doug comes."

"Before you go, will you find Jane and tell her to bring in the ripe tomatoes? I have to go to the store, and I'd like them in the kitchen and washed by the time I get back. I want to start canning before lunch."

"Got any idea where she is?"

"I saw her out the window about half an hour ago with her butterfly net, a paint brush, and a pail. I don't know where she is now."

Bill whistled through his teeth and shouted Jane's name, but there was no response. He walked once around the house without finding a clue. He heard the car start, then his father called, "I'm going to town with your mother. Have to pick up a spring for the baler. Stick around until we get back."

Bill untied Deer Fly, then wandered over to a large cottonwood at the southwest corner of the hayfield by the road. "We should keep Jane tied up like you, then we could find her when we want her."

Bill noticed that the goat was licking a sticky substance from the bark of the cottonwood. It darkened the trunk in a wide swath as though someone had painted it on with a brush. Insects seemed to be as much attracted to it as Deer Fly was, and quite a number of them floundered in it like little paratroopers who had jumped into quicksand.

The thought of old man Crawley surfaced in Bill's mind and with it the possibility of poison. He pulled Deer Fly away. "I'm not so sure you should be eating that stuff, Kid."

He fingered the coarse hair along the ridge of Deer Fly's backbone. He was puzzled. Deer Fly was provoked. She stamped a forefoot, and Bill heard it click against a hard object. He leaned over and picked up a peanut-butter jar. It contained a sprig of sweet clover and an orange-brown caterpillar curled in a furry circle on the bottom. "So that's it!" Bill exclaimed. "Another one of Jane's screwy ideas to catch bugs." He touched the sticky bark, looked at his finger, smelled it, then tasted it. "Yeah, molasses. No wonder you like it." He let go of the kid's collar and rubbed his hand on his jeans, then walked slowly to the road and turned south. He passed several more cottonwoods, then, just north of the Spook's woods—"Hey, Deer Fly, look. Another one." The kid was still engrossed in licking molasses from the first painted tree and hadn't noticed that Bill had left her behind. At his call, she galloped toward him like a rocket. When nearly on him, she gathered herself, reared, and with a careless toss to her head, struck the ground with her forefeet an inch from Bill's boot. "Think you can scare me, do you?" He rubbed her ears. She always liked that, especially when the flies were bad.

Bill continued on the road until he reached the Crawley woods. He had found no more painted trees. "Come on, Deer Fly. We've gone this way far enough." The goat was in no hurry. When Bill looked over his shoulder to see what was keeping her, he saw by the happy flicking of her tail that she had found more molasses.

"Another one!" Bill exclaimed. "I'll bet that crazy fool went to Crawley's. A fine time for her to run wild with Ma and Pa both gone. Now I've got to get her out of there. Pa'd want me to break my word this time. Can't let you go with me, though." He went back to his driveway and led Deer Fly to a fence post hidden from the road behind gooseberry bushes. He took off his belt, slipped it under the kid's collar, looped it around the fence wire and buckled it. "I'll be back quick as I can."

The kid's cries followed Bill as he continued through the woods. "Be quiet, Deer Fly. I'm just as lonesome as you, plus scared."

The marked trees were sometimes far apart, but most of them were near the road and led, as Bill suspected they would, toward the Crawley yard.

There was a thick growth of sumac and cedar at the northeast corner of the Crawley garden, allowing Bill to creep close without being seen. He sucked in his breath, then pulled to one side the cedar branch in front of him. Jane was there. She was examining a lilac bush between the garden and the road. He started to call her away, then checked himself as he caught a movement behind the house, about fifty yards from him.

It was the Spook. He carried a carton and walked toward the trash burner. As he moved, he kept looking over his shoulder, jerking his head like a squirrel's tail. It reminded Bill of that dusty couch, and he could imagine the Spook's mother laid out on it. *"She's a followin' me, and sometimes when I turn quick, I see her eyes a lookin' at me and a stick in her hand."*

Bill watched carefully as Crawley dumped the contents of the box into the wire frame and lit a match. It was apparently paper, and at first the flames flared; but after the first flash, the fire subsided to a thick smudge. Something in addition to paper was burning. When the breeze blew his way, it smelled like rotten meat charring. For some time Bill watched as Crawley jerked through the fog of smoke, apparently feeding the fire with sticks and rubbish that lay around the burner. Funny for him to get so neat all of a sudden, Bill thought.

After the fire had apparently burned down to his satisfaction, Crawley walked back to the house. Just before entering, he threw his arm over his head and ducked as though dodging a blow.

When the door closed behind Crawley, Bill called. "Jane." He spoke her name urgently as he stepped from behind the tree.

"That you, Bill?" She looked up from a lilac branch and twitched her head to send her braids down her back.

"Jane," he hissed.

"That's my name. Don't wear it out." She was relaxed as a cow in the noon sun.

"Come on out of there, but fast, or Crawley'll be after you."

"Are you nuts? All I'm doing is taking a few caterpillars off his lilacs."

"You know what Pa told you. He's crazy, and he'd go after just about anybody for just about anything. So come on right now, or I'll tell on you."

Jane started reluctantly toward Bill. "If I come now, promise you won't tell?"

"I promise. Now hurry on." As she came forward, Bill grabbed her arm.

"Stop dragging me. I've got burs all over my socks and they hurt."

"You can't stop here. Pull 'em out when you get home. I've got 'em too. Jane, don't you see? You gotta get out of here."

"You're just scared of the Spook, like when we were little kids."

"Sure I'm scared, and you would be too, if you knew enough to be."

"I wish I had a brother I could be proud of, not a scaredy-cat."

"At least I'm not scared of the dark," he jibed back.

"That's not as bad as being scared of a neighbor." Jane came to an abrupt halt. "My butterfly net! I've gotta go back and get it."

Bill let go of his sister's wrist and spoke with quiet authority. "Jane, you can't. I can't tell you why, but you just can't." She followed him.

Deer Fly bleated a welcome as the two approached her. "Okay, Kid. I'll untie you. Just hold on a minute." The goat was soon capering at their heels.

"When you came, I was just about through scouring the lilacs anyway. Look what I got." Jane took a peanut-butter jar from the shoulder bag she carried. In it were four Cecropia caterpillars.

"They're nice and big," Bill said.

When they were back in their own yard, Bill gave Jane his mother's message. He knew enough not to give it to her before he got her home. "Ma wants you to pick the ripe tomatoes."

"She would!" Jane went into the porch for a basket.

As Bill led Deer Fly to her stake, he noticed that the car was back and that Doug's bike was leaning against the porch.

"Hey, Bill, what's this stuff?" Doug shouted the question from the shade of the cottonwood where Bill had first noticed the painted bark.

"Molasses. Some crazy idea of Jane's," Bill said as he tied the rope to Deer Fly's collar and walked over to Doug.

"Brighty sure likes these bugs. Sort of like caramel apples." The jay was snapping up the sticky insects with relish. "Say, your pa says it's so late now that we're going to have lunch before we go over to Mr. Rutherford's."

"Yeah. I spent all this time chasing after that nutty Jane."

"Your ma says I can stay for lunch."

"Good. That'll save time."

After they finished eating, the boys trailed Mr. Brock to the

131

machine shed. "Can I drive?" Bill asked when the baler and wagon had been coupled onto the tractor.

"You know you can't drive off our place. I want you two boys on the rack." As Mr. Brock started the tractor, the boys climbed onto the bed of the wagon. They held to the uprights and stood as loose-jointed as the wagon they rode. Brighty perched on Doug's head, his feet tangled in coarse curls.

"I want to show Mr. Rutherford how Brighty can play dentist," Doug shouted over the roar of the tractor.

Mr. Rutherford had heard them coming and was opening the gate to the hayfield. "It's good of you and the boys to get this hay in for me, George."

"We have the time."

Mr. Rutherford smiled. "You mean you *make* the time."

"Your field is small. It won't take us long."

"Aw, we'll get that little bit done in no time," Doug chimed in. "I've got something to show you. Brighty's got a new trick."

"Fine. I'd like to see it, but perhaps you could save it until I get back. I have an appointment with sheriff Burnquist." He continued in answer to three questioning faces, "I had a cow stolen last night. She was only four years old and went reserve at Chicago last year."

"Oh no! Not your champion. I'm sorry to hear it. We won't keep you. Good luck." George Brock threw the tractor into gear and rolled toward the south field.

"Bet it was the Spook," Bill said.

"Yeah, and I'll bet we could catch Old Spook too. Wish we could get this hay in tomorrow."

"But we can't," said Bill. The baler was snatching up the windrows of hay, and Bill grunted as he picked the first bale from the ejection platform and heaved it onto the rack.

The dust and chaff clung to their sweaty skin and worked its way under their clothes. "I feel like I'm sharing my sleeping bag with a porcupine," Bill grumbled.

"Yeah, somebody sure thought up the right name when they called this rig a 'rack.' It's a torture spot all right."

When the whole field was baled and piled in the loft, most of the afternoon had slid by. The boys stopped off at Mr. Rutherford's barn for a drink of water, their dusty faces streaked with sweat, their lips outlined with rims of dirt. They drank and held their heads under the spigot.

"You boys look as though you've had a hot time of it."

They lifted their dripping heads and grinned at Mr. Rutherford, who was standing in front of them with two bottles of 7-Up and a can of beer for Bill's father. "That'll go pretty good," Doug said.

"Thanks," said Bill.

They sat on the stone wall in the shade of the barn and drank and talked. "Your hay cured just right," George said. "Green as you could want it and dry enough to keep from molding."

"Yes, it looks much better than last year's. Last winter I was feeding the cattle more stems than leaves. Alfalfa has to be cured just right."

Would they ever get to talking about the stolen cow? Mr. Rutherford seemed to have heard the unasked question. "Jim Burnquist spent about an hour searching the Crawley farm, but he couldn't find anything that would hold up in court. Now he's gone into town to check the stockyards. I gave him a picture of the cow and the number of her TB tag, but that's not much to go on."

"Anything hopeful?" George asked.

"Nothing yet. I don't have much hope. When I lost the heifer last spring, I thought it must be Crawley, but Mr. Burnquist and a deputy combed the premises. They didn't pick up a thing."

"It still might be Crawley. Would be a load off my mind if we could get him committed."

"Yes, I know," Mr. Rutherford went on. "But if it were he, why the best cow? He doesn't know a purebred from a scrub."

"It could be somebody who wants some good blood in their herd without paying the price."

"Maybe, but there was nothing special about the heifer that went last spring, and I suspect the same fellow took them both."

"Could be." George set down his empty beer can. As he did so, a call resounded from the sky, soon followed by the bold blue of its owner. He lighted on the can and gave the shining top a pecking.

"Well now, Doug, let me see that jay of yours perform."

"Okay, Mr. Rutherford. Here, Brighty, play dentist."

The bird fluttered to Doug's mouth and gave his bared teeth a vigorous drilling.

"Very good," Mr. Rutherford commended. "He really knows the meaning of your words—and the shine of your teeth."

"Gee, thanks." Doug reached into his pocket and paid his dentist with a raisin. The satisfied doctor flew to Doug's head to enjoy the fruits of his labor.

"That jay'll save your dad a lot of dentist bills," Mr. Rutherford said.

After a good laugh, George stood up. "Enough of this talk. It's time we were getting home. Good luck to you." George swung up to the tractor, and the engine noise drowned out Mr. Rutherford's parting words.

As they rattled past the Crawley place, Doug pointed toward the lilac hedge where a white cloth fluttered on the ground. "First time I've seen anything on the Crawley place that looked clean. Couldn't have been there long."

Bill's eye followed Doug's finger. *No, just since yesterday*, he thought, recognizing Jane's butterfly net.

"You know, we can't let Mr. Rutherford down," Doug said.

Bill wasn't listening. He was wondering what had gone into the Spook's trash burner. It smoked like garbage, but Crawley didn't burn his. He just threw it to the chickens.

"I know we could find a clue," Doug said as they pulled into the Brocks' yard.

When the boys hopped off the rack, Sammy was running to meet them. "Hey, look! Look what Ma got me in town." Eagerly he demonstrated the toy to the preoccupied older boys. It was a small kitten with a pink plush coat. When he wound it up, the whirling tail, which was curled over its back, rolled it over and over on the ground. Sammy gazed proudly at his possession revolving in the dust.

Doug gave it a passing glance. He was tired, and his shoulder muscles hurt. "So what?"

Bill didn't bother to look, but Bright Eyes didn't miss a movement. The toy slowed, then stopped. As Sammy leaned over to pick it up, the sun glinted on the key he held in his hand. From his vantage point on top of Doug's head, the jay swooped and snatched the glittering key. Sammy's tear-blurred vision followed Brighty's flight to the height of the barn roof.

"That's too bad," Bill sympathized. But Sammy was running too fast to hear the comforting note in his brother's voice. Bill picked up the kitten, dusted it off, and put it in his pocket.

"Poor little kid. He has it kind of rough," said Doug. "I should have said I liked the thing, but with all this stuff to think about, I just wasn't in the mood."

"Yeah. Sammy's sort of out of it." The boys stopped talking, and the high-pitched drone of cicadas formed a soundtrack for their thoughts.

Doug appeared to be getting an idea. Bill watched as his pal's face lit up. "Spill it," he said when, to all appearances, the idea was full blown.

"I just thought of something really great."

"Like those skunks?"

Doug ignored the taunt. "We can go over to the Spook's place tomorrow morning, and you can have a bunch of my cherry bombs and set 'em off in the woods. When Crawley goes off to look around, I'll sneak in and case the joint."

"That doesn't sound too good to me," Bill objected.

"What's wrong with it?" Doug challenged. "They blast like a gun."

"I don't know."

"You sound as if you don't even want to go."

Bill formed his objections slowly. "Trouble is the sheriff has already looked."

"Bill, you can't be yellow—not after all Mr. Rutherford's done for us?"

Bill kicked at a stone and fingered his case knife. There was no way he could back out without making Doug think he was a coward, unless he told him all he knew about Old Man Crawley, and that he couldn't do.

"How 'bout it? Are you a man or a mouse? Squeak up."

Doug's eyes were on him. Bill had promised his father, no way around that. But curiosity added its weight to his pride. What had gone into that trash burner? There was something else too. The more I run away, the more things seem to chase me, Bill thought. If I keep running from the Spook, maybe I will turn yellow. He kicked at a rock, still doubtful.

Bill looked toward the house. Sammy and Annie were crawling under the porch. That was it. Annie! There might still be a way out with honor. "I've got it," he said. "Let's go find Sammy."

"What do you want to do, play pin the tail on the donkey?"

"We're really going to need him."

"How the heck," Doug was muttering as he followed Bill to the house.

"Hey, Sammy," Bill shouted.

"Here I am," came a quiet voice at his feet. Bill looked down at his little brother wriggling out from under the porch. He was a dry, dusty color, but his smile was moist, and there was a moist dark line around his mouth and clean tear paths down his cheeks. He shook himself with a dog-like motion and stood up with his hand on Annie who had risen from the dust beside him.

"We need you and Annie." As he spoke, Bill was hoping that the border collie would abide by his father's training and stay off the Crawley place, but provide them a clue to what was on the Spook's land without going on it.

Sammy's wide eyes and white teeth looked remarkably clean. "How come?" he asked suspiciously.

Sammy couldn't be trusted to keep a secret. "I can't tell you now, but all three of us are going to meet tomorrow morning at eight o'clock. I'll be through at Mr. Rutherford's by then."

"Where?" Doug asked.

"Behind the silo."

"We'll be there." Sammy saluted.

"Bi-ill."

"That's Pa. I gotta do chores. See you tomorrow."

Chapter 15

The Search

"Spill it. I've been wondering all night," Doug said when he, Bill, and Sammy gathered behind the silo.

Sammy was looking around him as though he expected to see a fox's den or a two-headed turtle. "What are we here for?"

"We need Annie to track Mr. Rutherford's cow, and she won't work for me. I thought maybe she'd work for you," Bill said.

"Maybe." Pride mixed with doubt in Sammy's slow answer.

"Now I get it," said Doug. "But I still think cherry bombs are a good idea. I brought 'em along just in case. They'd distract the Spook big-time."

"Okay, but I don't think we'll need 'em. The Spook's bound to be either shocking oats or haying, and he won't come back in the middle of the morning."

"I suppose you're right. Let's get going."

"Okay," Bill agreed. "First we have to find where he got the cow out."

The boys started toward Mr. Rutherford's at a trot. They went up his driveway, then past the barn to the northwest corner of the cow pasture. "I think we ought to go straight south," said Doug.

Bill objected. "He'd hardly dare cut the fence right by the road."

"Okay. Guess that's right. We better go east."

The boys followed the line for only about fifty yards. Doug stopped. A low whistle quickly brought Bill and Sammy up with him. The four-strand fence had been freshly cut, and the bright ends hastily pulled together with baling wire. "Okay, set her on," Doug said to Sammy.

"Find the cow," Sammy said to the dog in a conversational tone. Annie looked quizzically into his face. He pointed to the wire, then to the ground. "Cow," he explained. Annie looked at Sammy as if she was a foreigner trying to understand English. Suddenly her tail began to wag, and she started to search the area with her nose.

"Let her start," Bill said to his brother.

"She's not in a hurry."

Impatiently the boys watched her careful sniffing. "She must have it by now," Bill said. "Get her started."

"Annie, we're going to find Mr. Rutherford's cow," Sammy explained to the dog.

"Not that way," Bill complained. "Tell her to *find* the way Pa does." Sammy and Annie turned back to the older boys, and Bill had the uncomfortable feeling that the white-snipped muzzle of the border collie was turned up in a sneer.

"Annie understands me just as well as Pa, and she minds me whenever she wants to."

"Yeah, when she *wants* to."

"She *does* want to. Finding's her favorite thing. If you don't like the way we do it, maybe we just won't go and find that old cow."

"Hurry up." Bill snapped with tension. "You can do it any way you like."

"We're going to find the cow, Annie," Sammy repeated. The

collie raised her ears, caught the word *find* and her name in Sammy's jumble, sniffed at the trail and moved carefully on. Her young friend's praise and faith were enough to keep the white feet moving steadily forward.

Sammy kept up a breathy whistle as he strode along with Annie, well ahead of the big boys. The trail led them to the road and across it. Annie and Sammy came to a halt at Old Man Crawley's fence.

"What are you stopping for?" Doug demanded, running up to Sammy and the dog.

Annie put her tail between her legs and crouched at Sammy's feet. "Don't run at her and talk so loud." Doug stepped back, and Sammy spoke to the dog. "Find the cow, please." Annie cast her eyes in the direction of the Crawley barn, but she would not move forward. "Pa won't let her go to Mr. Crawley's, so she won't go," Sammy said.

"Then make her." Doug jittered in place from one foot to the other.

"I can't make her do something when Pa says she can't."

"Too bad Brighty can't track, but we don't need to track any more. We know who took her," said Doug.

"Yeah, that's right." Bill nodded. It was obvious that Annie had no intention of leading farther.

"Now we need to find a good tree," said Doug.

"Huh?" Bill questioned.

"Yeah. To climb up and see where the Spook is."

"We shouldn't go to the Crawley place. We ought to call the sheriff," Sammy said, and Bill was inclined to agree.

"Not on your life!" Doug exclaimed with gusto. "Now that we've come this far, we're going to bring in the evidence. I'm heading for that old cedar up on the hill."

"I won't chicken," Bill said ruefully.

"Count me in," said Sammy.

With a chirp, Brighty fluttered from Doug's head to Bill's.

Annie looked toward home, then to the boys rolling under the fence. She hesitated, then, tail between her legs, she started trotting down the road toward home. "She's a good girl." Sammy followed her retreat with a guilty look.

"That's the trouble with her. No spirit of adventure. Brighty'll go anywhere." Doug ran toward the tree.

Sammy and Bill stood looking after Doug. "Come on," Bill said. "We gotta make our plans. Doug's halfway up the tree already." They followed to the far side of the cedar where they were protected by the feathery branches. Bill put his hand on Sammy's shoulder. "This might be dangerous," he cautioned. "You've got to do everything I say and *be quiet*. Don't forget."

"It doesn't look too good," Doug hissed down at them. "He's shocking in the oat field behind the house."

"Just our luck," Bill muttered. "But we can go around by the road and get in from the woods. That'll work, if we don't make a racket."

"Okay. Let's get going." Doug climbed down through the dense branches. The boys ran down the hill to the east, then north along the ditch beside the road, Sammy trailing.

"Hey, wait for me."

"You gotta hurry. We can't have any stragglers on this job."

"But I can't run as fast as you," he puffed.

"We never should have brought him," Doug hissed.

"But we'd better wait for him anyhow. It won't do to have him back there yelling."

Sammy was soon up with them, and they circled the outbuildings at a slower pace. "What are we looking for?" Sammy asked when he had caught his breath.

"Any sign of a Black Angus cow," Bill whispered. "I have a hunch about where to look for the TB tag."

"Give," said Doug.

"Follow me."

They had already gone by the machine shed and were approaching the south side of the barn. "Look," Sammy shouted. His sharp voice sliced the air. "There's a skeleton!" Doug and Bill pinned Sammy with their eyes.

"Go home," Bill whispered hoarsely. "Cross the road to Rutherford's, and go home on the other side. And *be quiet*." Sammy's face puckered as he turned and ran, sobbing, toward the road.

"Just that old calf skeleton, and he had to go wreck everything," Bill lamented.

"You stay here. I'll quiet him down," Doug said.

"Meet you in the machine shed," Bill whispered. "We better lay low and see what happens."

Sammy's wailing stopped and, in a few minutes, Doug joined Bill between a plowshare and the wall. "Sammy's alright now. I gave him something to do. But Crawley's coming. I saw him around the barn."

"You don't have to talk so loud." Bill's whisper was scarcely audible. "Did he see you?"

"I don't know."

For a long time the boys were quiet, listening. Bill got a cramp in his leg. When he straightened it out, his boot hit the plowshare, and the crack on metal sounded like a gun to the trapped boys. Bill felt Doug's hand tighten around his wrist, and he heard the sound, a steady tramp, coming closer. A silhouette filled the doorway, then started towards them. They were only partly hidden. As soon as Crawley's eyes adjusted to the dark, he would see them.

A sharp report cracked in the distance, like the opening day of hunting season—or the Fourth of July. With a jerk, the silhouette wheeled around, then disappeared from the doorway. Bill turned to Doug and saw him smile. "I take it back, what I said about those cherry bombs," Bill whispered when the sound of footsteps had faded. "Sure was lucky you thought of passing them on to Sammy."

"Not *luck*," Doug hissed.

The boys crawled to the door and looked out. A blow hit Bill on the back of the head. He flung up his hands and dropped to his belly. Doug and the jay were laughing together. Bill felt foolish. "That bird," he muttered. "I thought it was Crawley."

"I saw the creep go past the barn. He must be halfway to the woods by now."

"Hope so. I've had all I want." The boys walked toward the back of the house. Bill kicked the calf skull on the way by. They slunk around to the north side of the shed where a frayed rope dangled from the low branch of a dead tree. A dark stain on the ground brought a low whistle from Doug. "Yeah, I think what you think," Bill whispered. "Blood! But it doesn't *prove* anything. Come on." He led the way to the trash burner, picked up a stick and poked among the ashes. "The Spook was burning yesterday, and... Hey, what's this?" With his stick, Bill had uncovered a gray-white fragment of bone. A little more prodding, and he revealed the jawbone of a cow. "That's it. He butchered her and burned the head and guts. That beautiful cow!"

"We're really on track," Doug hissed. "You think she has a dental record?"

Bill was too scared to pay attention to a joke. "Yeah, but we still don't have the proof. Not without part of the hide, or the ear with the TB tag, or something."

"Guess you're right," Doug agreed. He found the handle of an old pitchfork and stirred the ashes. The boys searched in silence, their discouragement growing as their efforts failed to uncover any new clues.

"We better go home, huh?"

"Guess so, eh Brighty?" Doug rolled his eyes toward the bird on his head.

A gentle breeze found its way under a crumpled newspaper beside the trash burner. Brighty's restless eyes moved quicker than the paper. Something bright held his attention a moment, then he swooped to Doug's feet and snapped a piece of metal from the ground.

"The ear tag!" Doug exclaimed, holding out his hand for the jay. "Brighty, come." But Doug's happy exclamation died on his lips as Brighty soared over the tree tops in the direction of the Brocks' farm. The boys crossed the road, rolled under the white rails and ran after him through Rutherford's horse pasture.

"Are you sure it's the ear tag?" Bill panted. "All I could tell was that it was a piece of metal."

"I think so," Doug answered. "It was about the right size."

They ran the rest of the way to the Brocks' without talking. "I guess we really made a booboo this time," Bill said when he caught his breath.

"Yeah, Brighty did," Doug agreed. "The one time I really wanted him, and Brighty wouldn't come."

"That's how it goes."

The boys shuffled into the yard in low spirits. "Just when he was almost a hero, he flew out on me," Doug lamented.

The saucy jay picked that moment to drop to Doug's head—then, for just a moment, his owner came near swatting at him as though he were a fly. When he was met with no handout, the jay darted off again.

"Say, look." Doug called Bill's attention to the jay as he fluttered to the ground, scratched about in the leaves under the oak by the barn, then flitted to the roof with something in his beak. "It looks like he's picking up acorns and stowing them away under the shingles."

"That's what he did with the key to Sammy's cat, too."

"Yeah." Doug was running. "I'll bet that's what he did with the ear tag."

As were most of the trees in the Brock yard, the oak beside the barn was fitted with board steps up the trunk, and it didn't take Doug long to climb to the bottom branch. "Got a rope?" he called down. "If I had one, I could let myself down off this branch to the edge of the roof and then climb up."

"Have one in a minute," Bill called back and disappeared into the barn. He returned shortly with a manila rope, climbed up with Doug, then tied a square knot around the overhanging limb. In a few minutes they were on the roof, but it took them more than a few minutes to look under most of the shingles on the west side. Bill straightened up slowly, straddling the peak. "Boy, what a mess," he commented, looking at his fingers. "Looks like I got mixed up with a porcupine."

Bill looked down at the farmyard spread out like a model below him. It seemed artificially neat and well arranged. How would Deer Fly look from on top? He located the plum tree where he had tied her and looked under it. He saw the rope like a hair on a green rug. But at the end of it there was no kid.

Bill crawled down the steeply pitched roof and grabbed the rope. He shinnied up to the branch and climbed quickly to the ground. "Did you find it?" Doug was puzzled.

"No." Bill ran into the house. His mother was standing in the steam of a kettle of boiling tomatoes and ladling them into quart jars. "Ma, did you move Deer Fly to the old chain?" he asked hopefully.

"No, I didn't move her."

Bill turned to Sammy who was sitting at the kitchen table marking jars. He had finished sliding a label to a crooked halt and was nervously tearing another one into small pieces. "Did you untie her?" Bill accused.

"You sent me home."

With an effort, Bill held himself in check. "Has any car left the yard?"

Sammy answered in a whisper. "Just the meter man."

"Did he go north or south?"

"To Rutherford's, I think."

Bill took a step toward the door. Sadness overwhelmed Bill's anger. "You're a good kid, Sammy, but *why* did you do it?"

The screen door slammed. Bill heard the shiver of the spring closer long after the bang.

Chapter 16

Hog-Tied

A shortcut through the woods straight to the Crawley place would save time, but Bill decided in favor of sticking to the road. His worst fears could be wrong. If Deer Fly was browsing the brush along the road, it would be taking an unnecessary risk to chance being caught prowling around the Crawley farm, especially after what had just happened there.

As he walked down the road, Bill's was the direct stride of a man. His active mind was carefully channeled.

His eyes were fixed on the road and its borders. Bill noticed the bright blue of a jay against the somber green of a cedar growing under a telephone pole. The bird held his brazen position while Bill came close. "Is that you, Brighty?" The flashy bird dipped to his shoulder. "Glad you decided to come along. You can make as much racket as you like, and no one will be the wiser."

Bill moved cautiously through the brush that surrounded the Crawley yard. He was within seventy-five yards of the oat field where Crawley had been shocking earlier in the morning. A thicket of chokecherries and wild plum hid the edge of the field from his sight. He crawled through it until he could look into the field without being seen. He watched for a long time but saw no one.

He worked his way to the barn where a clump of cedars gave

cover. Bill had crept up to it and was about to stand when a shriek split the air. It sounded like the screaming of a baby, but Bill knew it for the cry of a terrified goat.

Brighty slipped from his perch on Bill's head and fell into the air when the boy shot forward.

He stood in front of the barn door. Bill knew his danger more clearly than he ever had before. In spite of, or perhaps because of knowing, he felt no fear, only the pounding rush of adrenaline. With a quick breath, he jerked open the loose-fitting door. His eyes, accustomed to sunlit vegetation, saw the interior as a blur of green. Dimly he made out a swinging form, and his hand went quickly to the case knife at his belt as he started forward. The sunlight from the open door was thrown back in his face from a shining strip of steel.

A butcher knife! Bill sidestepped to the left, away from the door, holding his knife behind him. His eyes had adjusted to the half-light, and Bill could now make out the interior of the barn clearly. Compared to his own, it was small. Two short rows of stanchions stretched away from him, homemade contraptions of wood that closed against the cows' necks when the upright was pushed so that a hinged block of wood dropped into place behind it. There were only three on each side. Across the back was a calf pen divided from the main part of the barn by a three-foot wall of planking. Bill noticed that it was occupied by at least one calf. There were two high windows on the south wall, but they were so festooned with dusty cobwebs that they let in little light.

Apparently the barn had not been cleaned for days. As Bill moved sideways, he was repulsed by the moist suction under his boots. He was opposite his kid now, and the light was coming through the door to his right. Deer Fly was convulsing and bleating futilely as she swung just clear of the ground, strung up by her hind legs to the horizontal two-by-fours over the stanchions. Her forelegs kicked vainly against the uprights, smooth and oily from the necks of generations of cows. Crawley had completed the knot and now had Deer Fly's head grasped under his left arm. The blade was ready to draw across the hide at the throat.

Crawley had the knife poised and was looking at the boy. He had not spoken. Bill noticed that the rope that bound Deer Fly was frayed, and one strand was broken. The grip of his knife was sticky in his hand as he moved forward.

Bill glided toward the stanchion, silent but for the moist sound of his footsteps. He kept his eyes on Crawley's face. As long as the old man's eyes were on him, he wouldn't draw the knife. For a moment the tattoo of Deer Fly's hoofbeats against the stanchion ceased. Her cries were quiet as she drew a breath. Bill crouched, his eyes still fixed to Crawley's face. The weight of silence snapped as Bill looked over Crawley's shoulder, then shouted, "Your ma! She's gonna get you!" Crawley threw his arms over his head, his knife slipped from his grasp, and he crumpled to the floor.

In the few seconds he had, Bill drew his knife blade through the rope that bound his kid's hind legs. She dropped to the ground, dazed for a moment. Bill touched her neck. "It's okay." The words were reassuring, but the tone tense. He started toward the door. Deer Fly quickly gained her feet and followed him. But Crawley was ahead of them blocking access to the door. Trapped! Only a crack of light remained. For a moment, a shadow blotted out the lower half of the door, and he thought he saw a flash of white. Was someone there? Bill thought he heard a sound, but it was too indistinct to classify. His hope was short-lived. He was alone in that barn with Crawley, and he had to help himself.

Bill backed toward the calf pen, putting as much distance as possible between himself and Crawley. He looked carefully for any possible means of escape. The windows were too high. He couldn't reach the door. Then Bill saw, in a shadowed corner between the calf pen and the north wall, a trapdoor to the loft. Leading up to it was something halfway between steps and a ladder. The rungs were about two inches wide, and laid up on a steep slope. The trapdoor to the loft was open. He could be up within three seconds, but what about the kid? She couldn't follow fast enough. He felt her shoulder close beside his leg. Crawley latched the door and started toward them.

"Deer Fly, up!" Bill's voice was sharp; as he spoke, he bounded between the stanchions to the base of the ladder. He knew the frightened goat would be reluctant to leave his side, but perhaps the habit of obedience would be stronger than her fear. She put a cloven hoof on the second step and looked at Bill. "Up," he repeated firmly. The familiar command was reassuring, and the goat climbed nimbly. Crawley had not reached the steps. Bill took no time to wonder why, but bounded up the ladder. As he reached the top, he heard the tearing of cloth, and a moment later he saw Crawley behind him, his jacket sleeve ripped from elbow to wrist. Bill had now gained the top and saw, to his dismay, that there was no trapdoor to close. As he turned to look down, his peripheral vision caught a flash in the open loft above him, too blue for a barn swallow. Bill had never seen a blue bird inside a barn. There was no time to think about it. Crawley was after him.

Most of the face below him was darkened in the shadow, but Crawley's eyes shone like cats' eyes at night. The butcher knife, gripped between his teeth, flashed the little light that filtered down. With his hands freed for climbing, Crawley was coming up fast. Bill could read murder on his face as clearly as if it had been a newspaper headline.

A bolt of blue shot to the glitter of the knife. Sharp-pointed leathery feet gripped Crawley's nose, and feathers fanned his eyes. The jay's alarm call and a shriek blended as Crawley fell backward to the floor. For a second Bill watched, but the old man

150

did not rise. His head had struck the top board of the stanchions. *If I could tie him while he's unconscious...* Bill went quickly down the ladder. Crawley's knife was on the floor about two feet to the right of his shoulder, and Bill took it and cut the rope from the stanchion. He first bound Crawley's feet. The hands should be tied behind his back, Bill knew, but Crawley was lying on his back, so that would not be easy. Rather than risk his regaining consciousness before the job was done, Bill tied Crawley's hands over his stomach. The scrawny wrists reminded him of the necks of plucked chickens.

"Deer Fly," he called. The kid picked her way down a couple of steps, then bounded to the floor of the barn and trotted lightly after Bill toward the door. He lifted the hook and let the door swing out. He paused a moment as a thin voice floated after him. "She got me this time, oooh, she got me." The voice suddenly rose to a sort of howl, then faded as Bill ran into the daylight.

He shut the barn door behind him, closing away the wailing voice. He filled his lungs with clean air and stood blinking in the sun. The kid rubbed her head against him, and he smiled down at her. "I was mad at you, Deer Fly, but I'm sure not now. Seems like everything I was scared of is behind me tied up in the barn, and you led me there." Bill recalled Mr. Rutherford's words: "Understanding can conquer your fear and make it helpless as a hog-tied steer." Bill wasn't so sure. Sometimes understanding made it worse. He walked toward the road with the kid beside him just as the Brock car came into sight.

"Bill, Bill!" Sammy burst from the back door. "Where's the Spook? What did he do?" His little brother's arms encircled Bill's legs before he could find an answer.

"Billy, are you all right?" His mother's words came in a worried volley. She and his father were running toward him.

"Sure I'm all right." He pointed over his shoulder. "Crawley's in the barn. I tied him up."

"You what?" His father was looking at him incredulously.

"Yeah, that's right. With a lot of help from Brighty and a board in just the right place."

"That'll take some explaining, but now I'd better go into the barn and take a look at your job."

"Hey, wait for me." It was Doug who had just come up on his bike and was hurrying after Mr. Brock. "I want to see him."

"Gee, you must be strong." Sammy was still standing with his arms around Bill's legs.

Bill rubbed his hair the wrong way and smiled down at him. "Nope. Just lucky. Say, where's Jane?"

"I don't know," his mother answered. "She was the one who called us. She had come here looking for her butterfly net and heard the kid bleating in the barn. She saw you go in and then ran home to tell us. But I'm surprised she isn't here. I thought she was in the car with us, but I can't be sure. I was too worried to look."

"Guess I'll run on home and find her. But first I gotta go back in the barn." It was hard to return into that dark stinky place, but he had to see what was happening with Crawley and his father. As he walked into the darkness, he felt cold and clammy with the fear he hadn't had time to notice when he was so busy dealing with the Spook. Now his father was in charge. Bill's eyes could make out the outline of his father's back looming over Old Man Crawley, who was still lying in the hay and manure on the slimy barn floor.

"You're going to be all right," Bill heard his father say to Crawley in a surprisingly gentle voice. "We're going to get some help for you quick as we can. That board split your head open pretty bad."

By the time Bill had walked up beside his father, his eyes had grown accustomed to the half-light filtering through the cracks of the barn. He could see the dark blood still pulsing from Crawley's thin hair to the floor under his head.

"It looks real bad," Bill said.

"Bill, I'm glad you're here. Will you tell your mother to call the hospital? This wound has to get cleaned out, and I'm sure it needs stitches."

As Bill went out to tell his mother, he didn't feel sorry about Old Man Crawley, only glad that it wasn't Deer Fly. After what he tried to do, the Spook sure deserved it.

Bill was relieved it was his mother, not he, going into Crawley's house to telephone the hospital. He never wanted to see that dump again.

His mother was shaking her head as she came out of the house. "Any person who lived in that hovel would have to be insane!" she exclaimed.

Bill felt a burst of anger and fear all mixed up. "Crawley sure is crazy, and I hope he rots in jail for the rest of his life!"

"Bill! That's no way to talk. I know you must be mad about what he tried to do, but wouldn't it be a lot better if he got some help and learned how to live with his fellow human beings?"

"I'm no 'fellow' of his," Bill mumbled.

"Whether we like it or not, we all have to live in this world together. The more we help each other, the better it will work out for all of us."

Bill tried kicking a half-buried stone out of the gravel of the driveway, but it wouldn't budge.

"Billy," his mother continued. "Do you realize how much you have helped Mr. Crawley?"

"Huh?" Bill stopped kicking at the rock.

"If all this hadn't happened, that poor old man might have gone on for years making every creature around him miserable, himself most of all."

"I sure never thought of that." Bill didn't have time to figure it all out before he heard the ambulance shrieking down the road. It backed up to the barn door, and two men got out the back with a stretcher. Bill thought of how it had been with his broken leg, and for the first time he thought of Crawley as a flesh-and-blood person.

As the paramedics came out of the barn, they had to tip the stretcher sideways to get it through the narrow door. Hearing Crawley moan, Bill almost felt sorry for all the pain he was in.

"He's still bleeding pretty bad," one of the paramedics said.

"Will he be all right?" Bill's father asked.

"Yeah, once they get him cleaned up and take a few stitches in his head."

Before he closed the ambulance door, the second man cautioned, "With a head wound like that, there's always danger of a serious concussion."

It seemed like less than two minutes before the ambulance was speeding back down the road, and Bill's parents and Sammy were getting back into the car. "Come on, Bill," his mother said.

"Sit by me!" Sammy exclaimed.

"Thanks, Sammy, but there isn't room for Deer Fly. We'll walk."

Bill walked a short way, then ran down the road with Deer Fly capering beside him. Feels good to cut loose, he thought. Kind of funny though, free, like when you've been packing a knapsack and then swing it off. The distance passed easily under his feet.

At the oak by the back porch, he stopped. He wouldn't have to look for Jane. She was standing by their mother, crying. "It's all right now, Jane. Look! Here's your brother, and he's perfectly fine."

Bill stood still, panting, and a little embarrassed. Jane didn't cry often, and never about him. Her head was down against her mother's shirt, and she still hadn't seen him. Bill felt more and more awkward the longer he stood silent. It appeared as though she wouldn't look up until he spoke. "What's the matter?"

"Oh Bill, you're really here. I was so scared I didn't dare look up." Their mother had left for the house when Jane continued. "When I peeked through a crack in the barn door, I saw him with that knife. I thought he'd kill you. That's why I stayed here. I couldn't stand seeing you all cut up. And I'm sorry."

"What for?"

"Just everything. I didn't understand."

"You're okay. Thanks for running home and trying to save me. Could have been real important."

Sammy strode up, a holster slapping against his thigh. "You needn't be scared. Bill had him all tied up when we got there."

"You can't stop being scared by running away," Bill said.

"That's right." Sammy had climbed up the steps so that he was tall enough to easily reach a hand to Bill's shoulder. "You gotta get in there and fight."

Bill smiled. "First you've got to know what you're fighting, and that's harder."

Doug had just pedaled into the driveway, and Bill's father was following. "I suppose Jane told you the good news," Doug panted.

"Nope, what is it?"

"Look." Doug was holding a small bit of metal. "3610584, the TB tag. I found it under a shingle near the ridgepole right after you left. Sammy's key, too."

"Aw, that kitten. I don't care about that any more. Got a new pistol." Sammy slapped the butt of his cap gun.

Doug saw that his news wasn't making much of an impression. "I guess the TB tag doesn't make much difference now," he said wistfully.

"Maybe not," Bill said, "but it sure is a good thing you taught Brighty to play dentist."

"And it's a good thing," said Mr. Brock, "that Old Man Crawley's on his way to the hospital. I felt ten years younger when that ambulance took him out of there."

"What about Brighty?" Doug reminded.

"When I went into the barn, Crawley was just about to butcher Deer Fly and..."

"I saw the knife," Jane interjected. "I thought he was going after Bill."

They all turned their attention back to Bill. "I cut Deer Fly down, but the Spook was standing by the door so I couldn't get out. Then I saw the steps to the loft, almost like a ladder. I told Deer Fly to climb up to the loft, and she did, and then I went up, and Crawley came after. I was up on top watching him come with a knife in his teeth, and I couldn't do anything about it. Then zoom goes Brighty, right for Crawley's knife, and the old crow's so surprised he falls over backwards and knocks himself out. Then all I do is tie him up."

"Gee," Doug breathed reverently. "Brighty sure is a hero."

"Mostly Bill's the hero," Sammy said. Jane nodded vigorously, and one of her pigtails fell forward. She twitched it back.

"Everybody's a hero," said their father, "and I'm taking you all for a swim and a double malt afterwards."

"Yippee!" Sammy exclaimed.

"I'd sort of like to stop and see Mr. Rutherford," Bill said.

"A good idea," said his father. "We'll stop on the way."

"I better get home and get my trunks." Doug grabbed the handlebars of his bike.

"Bill," Jane said timidly, "will you go with me tonight and look at my baits? I gotta go at night 'cause that's when the moths come, and I'm kind of scared in the dark."

Bill looked at her, but he didn't laugh. "Yeah, I know. I used to be scared of Old Man Crawley."

"I didn't believe what he was like until just today when I

156

saw him in the barn with that knife about to kill you and Deer Fly. I peeked through the crack in the door, but I didn't dare go in. How'd you do it? How'd you make your legs go?"

Bill remembered his long walk to the Cotherns' the day Deer Fly was born. "When you really know what you want, it helps a whole lot."

"I hear Doug already. You wait, and I'll get your suit for you." Jane ran to the clothesline as Doug rode into the yard.

"Gol. I can't wait to tell Mr. Rutherford what Brighty did."

"Yeah," agreed Bill. "I wish we'd gotten his cow back, though, instead of just the ear tag."

"Pile into the car, kids. We're on our way." Mr. Brock slid behind the wheel, and they were off.

Mr. Rutherford was saddling Sugar Foot when the Brocks drove into his yard. He came to meet them, hand outstretched. "Congratulations," he said as Bill took it.

"How'd you find out so soon?"

"News travels fast in this valley. But I haven't heard any of the details," he added, reading the disappointment in the boys' faces.

"Deer Fly led me there."

"I got Annie to track the cow, and she went to Crawley's... Almost."

"Brighty found the ear tag."

"Bill was the one who caught him," Jane said.

"Just a minute now. I can't listen to all four of you at once."

Bit by bit the story unfolded.

"...so Brighty saved Bill's life," Doug finished, "and Deer Fly's too."

"No, Doug, you did," Mr. Rutherford said. "You guided that bird's instinct as surely as the driver guides a car. Brighty could never have done it without you."

"Gee whiz, I never thought of that."

"And now, Bill," said Mr. Rutherford, "I have something I'd like to show you." He walked to the barn followed by Jane and the boys.

Back of a feed drum in the tack room was a small door. Mr. Rutherford rolled the drum to one side and opened it. The first thing the boys noticed was a cabinet gleaming with trophies and backed by satin ribbons. "Gee!" exclaimed Doug. "How come you never showed us all this before?"

Mr. Rutherford was standing by an angular object shrouded in a sheet. He looked back to see what Doug was referring to. "Oh, that was a long time ago. The present is more important, don't you think?" Mr. Rutherford went on without waiting for an answer,"I have something here I think you'll like, Bill." He pulled away the sheet.

The boys stared in mute wonder at an intricately carved and painted cart.

"My father brought this over from Sicily in 1896. When I was about the size of Sammy here, my pony pulled me in it." Mr. Rutherford lifted the shafts. "It's nicely balanced. On smooth ground I think Deer Fly could roll it easily."

"Gol!" Doug knelt between the shafts. "Say, look. Here's a bird painted blue. Not a jay though."

"And here is something else." Mr. Rutherford walked around the cart and pointed to some figures carved across the back. "See St. George killing that green dragon?"

"Golly, look. The dragon has two heads!" Bill exclaimed.

"Well, Bill, should we roll out your cart?"

Bill looked at Mr. Rutherford, unbelieving. "You mean it's for me?"

Mr. Rutherford picked up the shafts. "If you're going to graduate from stable boy to trainer," he said, "You need the proper equipment."

The sun blazed on the yellow cart, and the cart blazed back

at the sun, almost as bright. "There's room for two," Bill said to Doug.

From somewhere high up, a bird dropped—as blue and white as the sky and clouds it came from. Doug smiled. "Better make it three."